WAK

Returning from ⟨...⟩ Is neither painful nor ⟨...⟩re no sensations at ⟨...⟩ne temperature of a re⟨...⟩at time, though, an injection of nirvana flows within the body's thawed rivers.

It is only when consciousness begins to return, thought Mrs. Muller, to return with sufficient strength so that one fully realizes what has occurred—that the wine has survived another season in an uncertain cellar, its vintage grown rarer still—only then does an unpronounceable fear enter into the mundane outlines of the bedroom furniture. . . .

"What day is it?" she asked him.

"August eighteen, two thousand-two."

—from *The Graveyard Heart*, by Roger Zelazny

A NEW WRINKLE ON THE TOR DOUBLES

Along with our regular Doubles line of new and classic short novels of SF, Tor is also pleased to present a few Doubles made up of a classic by one SF author and an all-new companion piece by another. You'll be able to recognize these Doubles by their distinctive covers; other Tor SF Doubles will continue to feature the popular "flip-flop" format, with a separate cover on each side.

Both kinds of Tor SF Doubles will continue to bring you the finest short novels in the field—double doses of energy, ideas, and science-fictional excitement.

THE TOR SF DOUBLES

A Meeting with Medusa/Green Mars, Arthur C. Clarke/Kim Stanley Robinson • Hardfought/Cascade Point, Greg Bear/Timothy Zahn • Born with the Dead/The Saliva Tree, Robert Silverberg/Brian W. Aldiss • Tango Charlie and Foxtrot Romeo/The Star Pit, John Varley/Samuel R. Delany • No Truce with Kings/Ship of Shadows, Poul Anderson/Fritz Leiber • Enemy Mine/Another Orphan, Barry B. Longyear/John Kessel • Screwtop/The Girl Who Was Plugged In, Vonda N. McIntyre/James Tiptree, Jr. • The Nemesis from Terra/Battle for the Stars, Leigh Brackett/Edmond Hamilton • The Ugly Little Boy/The [Widget], the [Wadget], and Boff, Isaac Asimov/Theodore Sturgeon • Sailing to Byzantium/Seven American Nights, Robert Silverberg/Gene Wolfe • Houston, Houston, Do You Read?/Souls, James Tiptree, Jr./Joanna Russ • He Who Shapes/The Infinity Box, Roger Zelazny/Kate Wilhelm • The Blind Geometer/The New Atlantis, Kim Stanley Robinson/Ursula K. Le Guin • The Saturn Game/Iceborn, Poul Anderson/Gregory Benford & Paul A. Carter • The Last Castle/Nightwings, Jack Vance/Robert Silverberg • The Color of Neanderthal Eyes/And Strange at Ecbatan the Trees, James Tiptree, Jr./Michael Bishop • Divide and Rule/The Sword of Rhiannon, L. Sprague de Camp/Leigh Brackett • In Another Country/Vintage Season, Robert Silverberg/C. L. Moore • Ill Met in Lankhmar/The Fair in Emain Macha, Fritz Leiber/Charles de Lint • The Pugnacious Peacemaker/The Wheels of If, Harry Turtledove/L. Sprague de Camp • Home Is the Hangman/We, In Some Strange Power's Employ, Move on a Rigorous Line, Roger Zelazny/Samuel R. Delany • Thieves' Carnival/The Jewel of Bas, Karen Haber/Leigh Brackett • Riding the Torch/Tin Soldier, Norman Spinrad/Joan D. Vinge • Elegy for Angels and Dogs/The Graveyard Heart, Walter Jon Williams/Roger Zelazny • Fugue State/The Death of Doctor Island, John M. Ford/Gene Wolfe* • Press Enter ■ / Hawksbill Station, John Varley/Robert Silverberg* • Eye for Eye/The Tunesmith, Orson Scott Card/Lloyd Biggle, Jr.*

*forthcoming

WALTER JON WILLIAMS
Elegy for Angels and Dogs

The Graveyard Heart
ROGER ZELAZNY

A TOM DOHERTY ASSOCIATES BOOK
NEW YORK

THE GRAVEYARD HEART

Copyright © 1964 by Ziff-Davis Publishing Company

ELEGY FOR ANGELS AND DOGS

Copyright © 1990 by Walter Jon Williams

A Tor Book
Published by Tom Doherty Associates, Inc.
49 West 24th Street
New York, N.Y. 10010

Cover art by Bob Eggleton

ISBN: 0-812-50275-2

First edition: August 1990

Printed in the United States of America

0 9 8 7 6 5 4 3 2 1

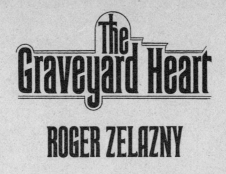

The Graveyard Heart

ROGER ZELAZNY

They were dancing,
   —at the party of the century, the party of the millennium, and the Party of Parties,
   —really, as well as calendar-wise,
   —and he wanted to crush her, to tear her to pieces. . . .

Moore did not really see the pavilion through which they moved, nor regard the hundred faceless shadows that glided about them. He did not take particular note of the swimming globes of colored light that followed above and behind them.

He felt these things, but he did not necessarily sniff wilderness in that ever-green relic of Christmas past turning on its bright pedestal in the center of the room—shedding its fireproofed needles and traditions these six days after the fact.

All of these were abstracted and dismissed, inhaled and filed away. . . .

In a few more moments it would be Two Thousand.

Leota (née Lilith) rested in the bow of his arm like a quivering arrow, until he wanted to break her or send her flying (he knew not where), to crush her into limpness, to make that samadhi, myopia, or whatever, go away from her gray-green eyes. At about that time, each time, she would lean against him and whisper something into his ear, something in French, a language he did not yet speak. She followed his inept·lead so perfectly though, that it was not unwarranted that he should feel she could read his mind by pure kinesthesia.

Which made it all the worse then, whenever her breath collared his neck with a moist warmness that spread down under his jacket like an invisible infection. Then he would mutter "C'est vrai" or "Damn" or both and try to crush her bridal whiteness (overlaid with black webbing), and she would become an arrow once more. But she was dancing with him, which was a decided improvement over his last year/her yesterday.

It was almost Two Thousand.

Now . . .

The music broke itself apart and grew back together again as the globes blared daylight. Auld acquaintance, he was reminded, was not a thing to be trifled with.

He almost chuckled then, but the lights went out a moment later and he found himself occupied.

A voice speaking right beside him, beside everyone, stated:

"It is now Two Thousand. Happy New Year!"

He crushed her.

No one cared about Times Square. The crowds in the Square had been watching a relay of the Party on a jerry-screen the size of a football field. Even now the onlookers were being amused by blacklight close-ups of the couples on the dance floor. Perhaps at that very moment, Moore decided, they themselves were the subject of a hilarious sequence being served up before that overflowing Petri dish across the ocean. It was quite likely, considering his partner.

He did not care if they laughed at him, though. He had come too far to care.

"I love you," he said silently. (He used mental dittos to presume an answer, and this made him feel somewhat happier.) Then the lights fireflied once more and auld acquaintance was remembered. A blizzard compounded of a hundred smashed rainbows began falling about the couples; slow-melting spirals of confetti drifted through the lights, dissolving as they descended upon the dancers; furry-edged projections of Chinese dragon kites swam overhead, grinning their way through the storm.

They resumed dancing and he asked her the same question he had asked her the year before.

"Can't we be alone, together, somewhere, just for a moment?"

She smothered a yawn.

"No, I'm bored. I'm going to leave in half an hour."

If voices can be throaty and rich, hers was an opulent neckful. Her throat *was* golden, to a well-sunned turn.

"Then let's spend it talking—in one of the little dining rooms."

"Thank you, but I'm not hungry. I *must* be seen for the next half hour."

Primitive Moore, who had spent most of his life dozing at the back of Civilized Moore's brain, rose to his haunches then, with a growl. Civilized Moore muzzled him though, because he did not wish to spoil things.

"When can I see you again?" he asked grimly.

"Perhaps Bastille Day," she whispered. "There's the Liberté, Egalité, Fraternité Fête Nue . . ."

"Where?"

"In the New Versailles Dome, at nine. If you'd like an invitation I'll see that you receive one. . . ."

"Yes, I do want one."

("She made you ask," jeered Primitive Moore.)

"Very well, you'll receive one in May."

"Won't you spare me a day or so now?"

She shook her head, her blue-blonde coif burning his face.

"Time is too dear," she whispered in mock-Camille pathos, "and the days of the Parties are without end. You ask me to cut years off my life and hand them to you."

"That's right."

"You ask too much," she smiled.

He wanted to curse her right then and walk away, but he wanted even more so to stay with her. He was twenty-seven, an age of which he did not approve in the first place, and he had spent all of the year 1999 wanting her. He had decided two years ago that he was going to fall in love and marry— because he could finally afford to do so without altering his standards of living. Lacking a woman who combined the better qualities of Aphrodite and a digital computer, he had spent an entire year on safari, trekking after the spoor of his star-crossed.

The invitation to the Bledsoes' Orbiting New Year—which had hounded the old year around the world, chasing it over the International Dateline and off the Earth entirely, to wherever old years go—had set him back a month's pay, but had given him his first live glimpse of Leota Mathilde Mason, belle of the Sleepers. Forgetting about digital computers, he decided then and there to fall in love with her. He was old-fashioned in many respects.

He had spoken with her for precisely ninety-seven seconds, the first twenty of which had been Arctic. But he realized that she existed to be admired, so he insisted on admiring her. Finally, she consented to be seen dancing with him at the Millenium Party in Stockholm.

He had spent the following year anticipating her seduction back to a reasonable and human mode of existence. Now, in the most beautiful city in the world, she had just informed him that she was bored and was about to retire until Bastille Day. It was then that Primitive Moore realized what Civilized Moore must really have known all along: the next time that he saw her she would be approximately two days older and he would be going on twenty-nine. Time stands still for the Set, but the price of mortal existence is age. Money could buy her the most desirable of all narcissist indulgences: the cold-bunk.

And he had not even had the chance of a Stockholm snowflake in the Congo to speak with her, to speak more than a few disjointed sentences, let alone to try talking her out of the ice-box club. (Even now, Setman laureate Wayne Unger was moving to cut in on him, with the expression of a golf pro about to give a lesson.)

"Hello, Leota. Sorry, Mister Uh."

Primitive Moore snarled and bashed him with his club; Civilized Moore released one of the most inaccessible women in the world to a god of the Set.

She was smiling. He was smiling. They were gone.

All the way around the world to San Francisco, sitting in

the bar of the stratocruiser, in the year of Our Lord Two Thousand—that is to say: two, zero, zero, zero—Moore felt that Time was out of joint.

It was two days before he made up his mind what he was going to do about it.

He asked himself (from the blister balcony of his suite in the Hundred Towers of the Hilton-Frisco Complex): *Is* this the girl I want to marry?

He answered himself (looking alternately at the traffic capillaries below his shoetops and the Bay): Yes.

Why? he wanted to know.

Because she is beautiful, he answered, and the future will be lovely. I want her for my beautiful wife in the lovely future.

So he decided to join the Set.

He realized it was no mean feat he was mapping out. First, he required money, lots of money—green acres of Presidents, to be strewn properly in the proper places. The next requisite was distinction, recognition. Unfortunately, the world was full of electrical engineers, humming through their twenty-hour weeks, dallying with pet projects—competent, capable, even inspired—who did not have these things. So he knew it would be difficult.

He submerged himself into research with a unique will: forty, sixty, eighty hours a week he spent—reading, designing, studying taped courses in subjects he had never needed. He gave up on recreation.

By May, when he received his invitation, he stared at the engraved (not fac-copy) parchment (not jot-sheet) with bleary eyes. He had already had nine patents entered and three more were pending. He had sold one and was negotiating with Akwa Mining over a water purification process which he had, he felt, fallen into. Money he would have, he decided, if he could keep up the pace.

Possibly even some recognition. That part now depended mainly on his puro-process and what he did with the money. Leota (née Lorelei) lurked beneath his pages of formulas, was cubed Braque-like in the lines on his sketcher; she burnt as he slept, slept as he burned.

In June he decided he needed a rest.

"Assistant Division Chief Moore," he told the face in the groomer (his laudatory attitude toward work had already earned him a promotion at the Seal-Lock Division of Pressure Units, Corporate), "you need more French and better dancing."

The groomer hands patted away at his sandy stubble and slashed smooth the shagginess above his ears. The weary eyes before him agreed bluely; they were tired of studying abstractions.

The intensity of his recreation, however, was as fatiguing in its own way as his work had been. His muscle tone *did* improve as he sprang weightlessly through the Young Men's Christian Association Satellite-3 Trampoline Room; his dance steps seemed more graceful after he had spun with a hundred robots and ten dozen women; he took the accelerated Berlitz drug-course in French (eschewing the faster electrocerebral-stimulation series, because of a rumored transference that might slow his reflexes later that summer); and he felt that he was beginning to *sound* better—he had hired a gabcoach, and he bake-ovened Restoration plays into his pillow (and hopefully, into his head) whenever he slept (generally every third day now)—so that, as the day of the Fête drew near, he began feeling like a Renaissance courtier (a tired one).

As he stared at Civilized Moore inside his groomer, Primitive Moore wondered how long that feeling would last.

Two days before Versailles he cultivated a uniform tan and decided what he was going to say to Leota this time:

—I love you? (Hell, no!)

—Will you quit the cold circuit? (Uh-uh.)

—If I join the Set, will you join me? (That seemed the best way to put it.)

Their third meeting, then, was to be on different terms. No more stake-outs in the wastes of the prosaic. The hunter was going to enter the brush. "Onward!" grinned the Moore in the groomer, "and Excelsior!"

She was dressed in a pale blue, mutie orchid corsage. The revolving dome of the palace spun singing zodiacs and the floors fluoresced witch-fires. He had the uncomfortable feeling that the damned flowers were growing there, right above her left breast, like an exotic parasite; and he resented their intrusion with a parochial possessiveness that he knew was not of the Renaissance. Nevertheless . . .

"Good evening. How do your flowers grow?"

"Barely, and quite contrary," she decided, sipping something green through a long straw, "but they cling to life."

"With an understandable passion," he noted, taking her hand which she did not withdraw. "Tell me, Eve of the Microprosopos—where are you headed?"

Interest flickered across her face and came to rest in her eyes.

"Your French has improved, Adam—Kadmon . . . ?" she noted. "I'm headed ahead. Where are you headed?"

"The same way."

"I doubt it—unfortunately."

"Doubt all you want, but we're parallel flows already."

"Is that a conceit drawn from some engineering laureate?"

"Watch me engineer a cold-bunk," he stated.

Her eyes shot X-rays through him, warming his bones.

"I knew you had something on your mind. If you were serious . . ."

"Us fallen spirits have to stick together here in Malkuth—I'm serious." He coughed and talked eyetalk. "Shall we stand together as though we're dancing? I see Unger; he sees us, and I want you."

"All right."

She placed her glass on a drifting tray and followed him out onto the floor and beneath the turning zodiac, leaving Setman Unger to face a labyrinth of flesh. Moore laughed at his predicament.

"It's harder to tell identities at an anti-costume party."

She smiled.

"You know, you dance differently today than last night."

"I know. Listen, how do I get a private iceberg and a key to Schlerafenland? I've decided it might be amusing. I know that it's not a matter of genealogy, or even money, for that matter, although both seem to help. I've read all the literature, but I could use some practical advice."

Her hand quivered ever so slightly in his own.

"You know the Doyenne./?" she said/asked.

"Mainly rumors," he replied, "to the effect that she's an old gargoyle they've frozen to frighten away the Beast come Armageddon."

Leota did not smile. Instead, she became an arrow again.

"More or less," she replied coldly. "She does keep beastly people out of the Set."

Civilized Moore bit his tongue.

"Although many do not like her," she continued, becoming slightly more animated as she reflected, "I've always found her a rare little piece of chinoiserie. I'd like to take her home, if I had a home, and set her on my mantel, if I had a mantel."

"I've heard that she'd fit right into the Victorian Room at the NAM Galleries," Moore ventured.

"She *was* born during Vicky's reign—and she *was* in her eighties when the cold-bunk was developed—but I can safely say that the matter goes no further."

"And she decided to go gallivanting through Time at that age?"

"Precisely," answered Leota, "inasmuch as she wishes to be the immortal arbiter of trans-society."

They turned with the music. Leota had relaxed once more.

"At one hundred and ten she's already on her way to becoming an archetype," Moore noted. "Is that one of the reasons interviews are so hard to come by?"

"One of the reasons. . . ." she told him. "If, for example, you were to petition Party Set now, you would still have to wait until next summer for the interview—provided you reached that stage."

"How many are there on the roster of eligibles?"

She shut her eyes.

"I don't know. Thousands, I should say. She'll only see a few dozen, of course. The others will have been weeded out, pruned off, investigated away, and variously disqualified by the directors. Then, naturally, *she* will have the final say as to who is *in*."

Suddenly green and limpid—as the music, the lights, the ultrasonics, and the delicate narcotic fragrances of the air altered subtly—the room became a dark, cool place at the bottom of the sea, heady and nostalgic as the mind of a mermaid staring upon the ruins of Atlantis. The elegiac genius of the hall drew them closer together by a kind of subtle gravitation, and she was cool and adhesive as he continued:

"What is her power, really? I've read the tapes; I know she's a big stockholder, but so what? Why can't the directors vote around her? If I paid out—"

"They *wouldn't*," she said. "Her money means nothing. She is an institution.

"Hers is the quality of exclusiveness which keeps the Set the Set," she went on. "Imitators will always fail because they lack her discrimination. They'll take in any boorish body who'll pay. *That* is the reason that People Who Count," (she pronounced the capitals), "will neither attend nor sponsor any but Set functions. All exclusiveness would vanish from the Earth if the Set lowered its standards."

"Money is money," said Moore. "If others paid the same for their parties . . ."

". . . Then the People who take their money would cease to Count. The Set would boycott them. They would lose their élan, be looked upon as hucksters."

"It sounds like a rather vicious moebius."

"It is a caste system with checks and balances. Nobody really wants it to break down."

"Even those who wash out?"

"Silly! They'd be the last. There's nothing to stop them from buying their own bunkers, if they can afford it, and waiting another five years to try again. They'd be wealthier anyhow for the wait, if they invest properly. Some have waited decades, and are still waiting. Some have made it after years of persisting. It makes the game more interesting, the achievement more satisfying. In a world of physical ease, brutal social equality, and reasonable economic equality, exclusiveness in frivolity becomes the most sought-after of all distinctions."

" 'Commodities,' " he corrected.

"No," she stated, "it is not for sale. Try buying it if money is all you have to offer."

That brought his mind back to more immediate considerations.

"What *is* the cost, if all the other qualifications are met?"

"The rule on that is sufficiently malleable to permit an otherwise qualified person to meet his dues. He guarantees his tenure, bunk-wise or Party-wise, until such a time as his income offsets his debt. So if he only possesses a modest fortune, he may still be quite eligible. This is necessary if we are to preserve our democratic ideals."

She looked away, looked back.

"Usually a step-scale of percentages on the returns from his investments is arranged. In fact, a Set counselor will be right there when you liquidate your assets, and he'll recommend the best conversions."

"Set must clean up on this."

"*Certainement*. It *is* a business, and the Parties don't come cheaply. But then, you'd be a part of Set yourself—being a shareholder is one of the membership requirements—and we're a restricted corporation, paying high dividends. Your principal will grow. If you were to be accepted, join, and then quit after even one objective month, something like twenty actual years would have passed. You'd be a month older and much wealthier when you leave—and perhaps somewhat wiser."

"Where do I go to put my name on the list?"

He knew, but he had hopes.

"We can call it in tonight, from here. There is always someone in the office. You will be visited in a week or so, after the preliminary investigation."

"Investigation?"

"Nothing to worry about. Or have you a criminal record, a history of insanity, or a bad credit rating?"

Moore shook his head.

"No, no, and no."

"Then you'll pass."

"But will I actually have a chance of getting in, against all those others?"

It was as though a single drop of rain fell upon his chest.

"Yes," she replied, putting her cheek into the hollow of his neck and staring out over his shoulder so that he could not see her expression, "you'll make it all the way to the lair of Mary Maude Mullen with a member sponsoring you. That final hurdle will depend on yourself."

"Then I'll make it," he told her.

". . . The interview may only last seconds. She's quick; her decisions are almost instantaneous, and she's never wrong."

"Then I'll make it," he repeated, exulting.

Above them, the zodiac rippled.

Moore found Darryl Wilson in a barmat in the Poconos. The actor had gone to seed; he was not the man Moore remembered from the award-winning frontier threelie series. That man had been a crag-browed, bushy-faced Viking of the prairies. In four years' time a facial avalanche had occurred, leaving its gaps and runnels across his expensive frown and dusting the face fur a shade lighter. Wilson had left it that way and cauterized his craw with the fire water he had denied the Red Man weekly. Rumor had it he was well into his second liver.

Moore sat beside him and inserted his card into the counter slot. He punched out a Martini and waited. When he noticed that the man was unaware of his presence, he observed, "You're Darryl Wilson and I'm Alvin Moore. I want to ask you something."

The straight-shooting eyes did not focus.

"News media man?"

"No, an old fan of yours," he lied.

"Ask away then," said the still-familiar voice. "You are a camera."

"Mary Maude Mullen, the bitch-goddess of the Set," he said. "What's she like?"

The eyes finally focused.

"You up for deification this session?"

"That's right."

"What do you think?"

Moore waited, but there were no more words, so he finally asked, "About what?"

"Anything. You name it."

Moore took a drink. He decided to play the game if it would make the man more tractable.

"I think I like Martinis," he stated. "Now—"

"Why?"

Moore growled. Perhaps Wilson was too far gone to be of any help. Still, one more try . . .

"Because they're relaxing and bracing, both at the same time, which is something I need after coming all this way."

"Why do you want to be relaxed and braced?"

"Because I prefer it to being tense and unbraced."

"Why?"

"What the hell is all this?"

"You lose. Go home."

Moore stood.

"Suppose I go out again and come back in and we start over? Okay?"

"Sit down. My wheels turn slowly but they still turn," said Wilson. "We're talking about the same thing. You want to know what Mary Maude is like. That's what she's like— all interrogatives. Useless ones. Attitudes are a disease that no one's immune to, and they vary so easily in the same person. In two minutes she'll have you stripped down to them, and your answers will depend on biochemistry and the weather. So will her decision. There's nothing I can tell you. She's pure caprice. She's life. She's ugly."

"That's all?"

"She refuses the wrong people. That's enough. Go away."

Moore finished his Martini and went away.

That winter Moore made a fortune. A modest one, to be sure.

He quit his job for a position with the Akwa Mining Research Lab, Oahu Division. It added ten minutes to his commuting time, but the title, Processing Director, sounded better than Assistant Division Chief, and he was anxious for a new sound. He did not slacken the pace of his force-fed social acceptability program, and one of its results was a January lawsuit.

The Set, he had been advised, preferred divorced male candidates to the perpetually single sort. For this reason, he had consulted a highly-rated firm of marriage contractors and entered into a three-month renewable, single partner drop-option contract, with Diane Demetrios, an unemployed model of Greek-Lebanese extraction.

One of the problems of modeling, he decided later, was that there were too many surgically-perfected female eidolons in the labor force; it was a rough profession in which to stay employed. His newly-acquired status had been sufficient inducement to cause Diane to press a breach of promise suit on the basis of an alleged oral agreement that the option *would* be renewed.

Burgess Social Contracting Services of course sent a properly obsequious adjuster, and they paid the court costs as well as the medfees for Moore's broken nose. (Diane had hit him with *The Essentials of Dress Display*, a heavy, illustrated talisman of a manual, which she carried about in a plastic case—as he slept beside their pool—plastic case and all.)

So, by the month of March Moore felt ready and wise and capable of facing down the last remaining citizen of the nineteenth century.

By May, though, he was beginning to feel he had overtrained. He was tempted to take a month's psychiatric leave from his work, but he recalled Leota's question about a history of insanity. He vetoed the notion and thought of Leota. The world stood still as his mind turned. Guiltily, he realized that he had not thought of her for months. He had been too busy with his autodidactics, his new job, and Diane Demetrios to think of the Setqueen, his love.

He chuckled.

Vanity, he decided; I want her because everyone wants her. No, that wasn't true either, exactly. . . . He wanted—what? He thought upon his motives, his desires.

He realized, then, that his goals had shifted; the act had become the actor. What he really wanted, first and foremost, impure and unsimple, was an in to the Set—that century-spanning stratocruiser, luxury class, jetting across tomorrow and tomorrow and all the days that followed after—to ride high, like those gods of old who appeared at the rites of the equinoxes, slept between precessions, and were remanifest with each new season, the bulk of humanity living through all those dreary days that lay between. To be a part of Leota was to be a part of the Set, and that was what he wanted now. So of course it was vanity. It was love.

He laughed aloud. His autosurf initialed the blue lens of the Pacific like a manned diamond, casting the sharp cold chips of its surface up and into his face.

Returning from absolute zero, Lazarus-like, is neither painful nor disconcerting, at first. There are no sensations at all until one achieves the temperature of a reasonably warm corpse. By that time though, an injection of nirvana flows within the body's thawed rivers.

It is only when consciousness begins to return, thought Mrs. Mullen, to return with sufficient strength so that one fully realizes what has occurred—that the wine has survived another season in an uncertain cellar, its vintage grown rarer still—only then does an unpronounceable fear enter into the mundane outlines of the bedroom furniture—for a moment.

It is more a superstitious attitude than anything, a mental quaking at the possibility that the stuff of life, one's own life, has in some indefinable way been tampered with. A microsecond passes, and then only the dim recollection of a bad dream remains.

She shivered, as though the cold was still locked within her bones, and she shook off the notion of nightmares past.

She turned her attention to the man in the white coat who stood at her elbow.

"What day is it?" she asked him.

He was a handful of dust in the winds of Time. . . .

"August eighteen, two thousand-two," answered the handful of dust. "How do you feel?"

"Excellent, thank you," she decided. "I've just touched upon a new century—this makes three I've visited—so why shouldn't I feel excellent? I intend to visit many more."

"I'm sure you will, madam."

The small maps of her hands adjusted the counterpane. She raised her head.

"Tell me what is new in the world."

The doctor looked away from the sudden acetylene burst behind her eyes.

"We have finally visited Neptune and Pluto," he narrated.

"They are quite uninhabitable. It appears that man is alone in the solar system. The Lake Sahara project has run into more difficulties, but it seems that work may begin next spring now that those stupid French claims are near settlement. . . ." Her eyes fused his dust to planes of glass.

"Another competitor, Futuretime Gay, entered into the time-tank business three years ago," he recited, trying to smile, "but we met the enemy and they are ours—Set bought them out eight months ago. By the way, our own bunkers are now much more sophistica—"

"I repeat," she said, "what is new in the world, *doctor*?"

He shook his head, avoiding the look she gave him.

"We can lengthen the remissions now," he finally told her, "quite a time beyond what could be achieved by the older methods."

"A better delaying action?"

"Yes."

"But not a cure?"

He shook his head.

"In my case," she told him, "it has already been abnormally delayed. The older nostrums have already worn thin. For how long are the new ones good?"

"We still don't know. You have an unusual variety of M.S. and it's complicated by other things."

"Does a cure seem any nearer?"

"It could take another twenty years. We might have one tomorrow."

"I see." The brightness subsided. "You may leave now, young man. Turn on my advice tape as you go."

He was glad to let the machine take over.

Diane Demetrios dialed the library and requested the Set-book. She twirled the page-dial and stopped.

She studied the screen as though it were a mirror, her face undergoing a variety of expressions.

"I look just as good," she decided after a time. "Better, even. Your nose could be changed, and your browline . . .

"If they weren't facial fundamentalists," she told the picture, "If they didn't discriminate against surgery, lady—you'd be here and I'd be there.

"Bitch!"

The millionth barrel of converted seawater emerged, fresh and icy, from the Moore Purifier. Splashing from its chamber-tandem and flowing through the conduits, it was clean, useful, and singularly unaware of these virtues. Another transfusion of briny Pacific entered at the other hand.

The waste products were used in pseudoceramicware.

The man who designed the doubleduty Purifier was rich.

The temperature was 82° in Oahu.

The million-first barrel splashed forth. . . .

They left Alvin Moore surrounded by china dogs.

Two of the walls were shelved, floor to ceiling. The shelves were lined with blue, green, pink, russet (not to mention ochre, vermilion, mauve, and saffron) dogs, mainly glazed (although some were dry-rubbed primitives), ranging from the size of a largish cockroach up to that of a pigmy warthog. Across the room a veritable Hadès of a wood fire roared its metaphysical challenge into the hot July of Bermuda.

Set above it was a mantelpiece bearing more dogs.

Set beside the hellplace was a desk, at which was seated Mary Maude Mullen, wrapped in a green and black tartan. She studied Moore's file, which lay open on the blotter. When she spoke to him she did not look up.

Moore stood beside the chair which had not been offered him and pretended to study the dogs and the heaps of Georgian kindling that filled the room to overflowing.

While not overly fond of live dogs, Moore bore them no malice. But when he closed his eyes for a moment he experienced a feeling of claustrophobia.

These were not dogs. These were the unblinking aliens staring through the bars of the last Earthman's cage. Moore promised himself that he would say nothing complimentary about the garish rainbow of a houndpack (fit, perhaps, for stalking a jade stag the size of a Chihuahua); he decided it could only have sprung from the mental crook of a monomaniac, or one possessed of a very feeble imagination and small respect for dogs.

After verifying all the generalities listed on his petition, Mrs. Mullen raised her pale eyes to his.

"How do you like my doggies?" she asked him.

She sat there, a narrow-faced, wrinkled woman with flaming hair, a snub nose, an innocent expression, and the lingering twist of the question quirking her thin lips.

Moore quickly played back his last thoughts and decided to maintain his integrity in regards china dogs by answering objectively.

"They're quite colorful," he noted.

This was the wrong answer, he felt, as soon as he said it. The question had been too abrupt. He had entered the study ready to lie about anything but china dogs. So he smiled.

"There are a dreadful lot of them about. But of course they don't bark or bite or shed, or do other things. . . ."

She smiled back.

"My dear little, colorful little bitches and sons of bitches," she said. "They don't do anything. They're sort of symbolic. That's why I collect them too.

"Sit down"—she gestured—"and pretend you're comfortable."

"Thanks."

"It says here that you rose only recently from the happy ranks of anonymity to achieve some sort of esoteric distinction in the sciences. Why do you wish to resign it now?"

"I wanted money and prestige, both of which I was given to understand would be helpful to a Set candidate."

"Aha! Then they were a means rather than an end?"

"That is correct."

"Then tell me why you want to join the Set."

He had written out the answer to that one months ago. It had been bake-ovened into his brain, so that he could speak it with natural inflections. The words began forming themselves in his throat, but he let them die there. He had planned them for what he had thought would be maximum appeal to a fan of Tennyson's. Now he was not so sure.

Still . . . He broke down the argument and picked a neutral point—the part about following knowledge like a sinking star.

"There will be a lot of changes over the next several decades. I'd like to see them with a young man's eyes."

"As a member of the Set you will exist more to be seen than to see," she replied, making a note in his file. ". . . And I think we'll have to dye your hair if we accept you."

"The hell you say! —Pardon me, that slipped out."

"Good." She made another note. "We can't have them too inhibited—nor too uninhibited, for that matter. Your reaction was rather quaint." She looked up again.

"Why do you want so badly to see the future?"

He felt uneasy. It seemed as though she knew he was lying.

"Plain human curiosity," he answered weakly, "as well as some professional interest. Being an engineer—"

"We're not running a seminar," she observed. "You'd not be wasting much time outside of attending Parties if you wanted to last very long with the Set. In twenty years—no, ten—you'll be back in kindergarten so far as engineering is concerned. It will all be hieroglyphics to you. You don't read hieroglyphics, do you?"

He shook his head.

"Good," she continued, "I have an inept comparison.— Yes, it will all be hieroglyphics, and if you should leave the Set you would be an unskilled draftsman—not that you'd have need to work. But if you were to want to work, you would have to be self-employed—which grows more and more difficult, almost too difficult to attempt, as time moves on. You would doubtless lose money."

He shrugged and raised his palms. He *had* been thinking of doing that. Fifty years, he had told himself, and we could kick the Set, be rich, and I could take refresher courses and try for a consultantship in marine engineering.

"I'd know enough to appreciate things, even if I couldn't participate," he explained.

"You'd be satisfied just to observe?"

"I think so," he lied.

"I doubt it." Her eyes nailed him again. "Do you think you are in love with Leota Mason? She nominated you, but of course that *is* her privilege."

"I don't know," he finally said. "I thought so at first, two years ago. . . ."

"Infatuation is fine," she told him. "It makes for good gossip. Love, on the other hand, I will not tolerate. Purge yourself of such notions. Nothing is so boring and ungay at a Set affair. It does not make for gossip; it makes for snickers.

"So is it infatuation or love?"

"Infatuation," he decided.

She glanced into the fire, glanced at her hands.

"You will have to develop a Buddhist's attitude toward the world around you. That world will change from day to day. Whenever you stop to look at it, it will be a different world—unreal."

He nodded.

"Therefore, if you are to maintain your stability, the Set must be the center of all things. Wherever your heart lies, there also shall reside your soul."

He nodded again.

". . . And if you should happen not to like the future, whenever you do stop to take a look at it, remember, you *cannot* come back. Don't just think about that, *feel* it!"

He felt it.

She began jotting. Her right hand began suddenly to tremble. She dropped the pen and too carefully drew her hand back within the shawl.

"You are not so colorful as most candidates," she told him, too naturally, "but then, we're short on the soulful type at present. Contrast adds depth and texture to our displays. Go view all the tapes of our past Parties."

"I already have."

". . . And you can give your soul to that, or a significant part thereof?"

"Wherever my heart lies . . ."

"In that case, you may return to your lodgings, Mister Moore. You will receive our decision today."

Moore stood. There were so many questions he had not been asked, so many things he had wanted to say, had forgotten, or had not had opportunity to say. . . . Had she already decided to reject him? he wondered. Was that why the interview had been so brief? Still, her final remarks *had* been encouraging.

He escaped from the fragile kennel, all his pores feeling like fresh nail holes.

He lolled about the hotel pool all afternoon, and in the evening he moved into the bar. He did not eat dinner.

When he received the news that he had been accepted, he was also informed by the messenger that a small gift to his inquisitor was a thing of custom. Moore laughed drunkenly, foreseeing the nature of the gift.

Mary Maude Mullen received her first Pacificware dog from Oahu with a small, sad shrug that almost turned to a shudder. She began to tremble then, nearly dropping it from her fingers. Quickly, she placed it on the bottommost shelf behind her desk and reached for her pills; later, the flames caused it to crack.

They were dancing. The sea was an evergreengold sky above the dome. The day was strangely young.

Tired remnants of the Party's sixteen hours, they clung to one another, feet aching, shoulders sloped. There were eight couples still moving on the floor, and the weary musicians fed them the slowest music they could make. Sprawled at the edges of the world, where the green bowl of the sky joined with the blue tiles of the Earth, some five hundred people, garments loosened, mouths open, stared liked goldfish on a tabletop at the water behind the wall.

"Think it'll rain?" he asked her.

"Yes," she answered.

"So do I. So much for the weather. Now, about that week on the moon—?"

"What's wrong with good old mother Earth?" she smiled.

Someone screamed. The sound of a slap occurred almost simultaneously. The screaming stopped.

"I've never been to the moon," he replied.

She seemed faintly amused.

"I have. I don't like it."

"Why?"

"It's the cold, crazy lights outside the dome," she said, "and the dark, dead rocks everywhere around the dome," she winced. "They make it seem like a cemetery at the end of Time. . . ."

"Okay," he said, "forget it."

". . . And the feeling of disembodied lightness as you move about inside the dome—"

"All right!"

"I'm sorry." She brushed his neck with her lips. He touched her forehead with his. "The Set has lost its shellac," she smiled.

"We're not on tape anymore. It doesn't matter now."

A woman began sobbing somewhere near the giant sea-horse that had been the refreshment table. The musicians played more loudly. The sky was full of luminescent starfish, swimming moistly on their tractor beams. One of the starfish dripped salty water on them as it passed overhead.

"We'll leave tomorrow," he said.

"Yes, tomorrow," she said.

"How about Spain?" he said. "This is the season of the sherries. There'll be the Juegos Florales de la Vendimia Jerezana. It may be the last."

"Too noisy," she said, "with all those fireworks."

"But gay."

"Gay," she sighed with a crooked mouth. "Let's go to Switzerland and pretend we're old, or dying of something romantic."

"Necrophilist," he grinned, slipping on a patch of moisture and regaining his balance. "Better it be a quiet loch in the Highlands, where you can have your fog and miasma and I can have my milk and honeydew unblended."

"Nay," she said, above a quick babble of drunken voices, "let's go to New Hampshire."

"What's wrong with Scotland?"

"I've never been to New Hampshire."

"I have, and *I* don't like it. It looks like your description of the moon."

A moth brushing against a candle flame, the tremor.

The frozen bolt of black lightning lengthened slowly in the green heavens. A sprinkling of soft rain began.

As she kicked off her shoes he reached out for a glass on the floating tray above his left shoulder. He drained it and replaced it.

"Tastes like someone's watering the drinks."

"Set must be economizing," she said.

Moore saw Unger then, glass in hand, standing at the edge of the floor watching them.

"I see Unger."

"So do I. He's swaying."

"So are we," he laughed.

The fat bard's hair was a snowy chaos and his left eye was swollen nearly shut. He collapsed with a bubbling murmur, spilling his drink. No one moved to help him.

"I believe he's overindulged himself again."

"Alas, poor Unger," she said without expression, "I knew him well."

The rain continued to fall and the dancers moved about the floor like the figures in some amateur puppet show.

"They're coming!" cried a non-Setman, crimson cloak flapping. "They're coming down!"

The water streamed into their eyes as every conscious head in the Party Dome was turned upward. Three silver zeppelins grew in the cloudless green.

"They're coming for us," observed Moore.

"They're going to make it!"

The music had paused momentarily, like a pendulum at the end of its arc. It began again.

Good night, ladies, played the band, *good night, ladies . . .*

"We're going to live!"

"We'll go to Utah," he told her, eyes moist, "where they don't have seaquakes and tidal waves."

Good night ladies . . .

"We're going to live!"

She squeezed his hand.

"Merrily we roll along," the voices sang, *"roll along . . ."*

" 'Roll along,' " she said.

" 'Merrily,' " he answered.

"O'er the deep blue sea!"

A Set-month after the nearest thing to a Set disaster on record (that is to say, in the year of Our Lord and President Cambert 2019, twelve years after the quake), Setman Moore and Leota (née Lachesis) stood outside the Hall of Sleep on Bermuda Island. It was almost morning.

"I believe I love you," he mentioned.

"Fortunately, love does not require an act of faith," she noted, accepting a light for her cigar, "because I don't believe in anything."

"Twenty years ago I saw a lovely woman at a Party and I danced with her."

"Five weeks ago," she amended.

"I wondered then if she would ever consider quitting the Set and going human again, and being heir to mortal ills."

"I have often wondered that myself," she said, "in idle moments. But she won't do it. Not until she is old and ugly."

"That means forever," he smiled sadly.

"You *are* noble." She blew smoke at the stars, touched the cold wall of the building. "Someday, when people no longer look at her, except for purposes of comparison with some fluffy child of the far future—or when the world's standards of beauty have changed—then she'll transfer from the express run to the local and let the rest of the world go by."

"Whatever the station, she will be all alone in a strange town," said Moore. "Every day, it seems, they remodel the world. I met a fraternity brother at that dinner last night— pardon me, last year—and he treated me as if he were my father. His every other word was 'son' or 'boy' or 'kid,' and he wasn't trying to be funny. He was responding to what he saw. My appetite was considerably diminished."

"Do you realize where we're going?" he asked the back of her head as she turned away to look out over the gardens of sleeping flowers. "Away! That's where. We can never go back! The world moves on while we sleep."

"Refreshing, isn't it?" she finally said. "And stimulating, and awe-inspiring. Not being bound, I mean. Everything burning. Us remaining. Neither time nor space can hold us, unless we consent.

"And I do not consent to being bound," she declared.

"To anything?"

"To anything."

"Supposing it's all a big joke."

"What?"

"The world. —Supposing every man, woman, and child died last year in an invasion by creatures from Alpha Centauri, everyone but the frozen Set. Supposing it was a totally effective virus attack. . . . ''

"There are no creatures in the Centauri System. I read that the other day."

"Okay, someplace else then. Supposing all the remains and all the traces of chaos were cleaned up, and then one creature gestured with a flipper at this building." Moore slapped the wall. "The creature said: 'Hey! There are some live ones inside, on ice. Ask one of the sociologists whether they're worth keeping, or if we should open the refrigerator door and let them spoil.' Then one of the sociologists came and looked at us, all in our coffins of ice, and *he* said: 'They might be worth a few laughs and a dozen pages in an obscure periodical. So let's fool them into thinking that everything is going on just as it was before the invasion. All their movements, according to these schedules, are preplanned, so it shouldn't be too difficult. We'll fill their Parties with human simulacra packed with recording machinery and we'll itemize their behavior patterns. We'll vary their circumstances and they'll attribute it to progress. We can watch them perform in all sorts of situations that way. Then, when we're finished, we can always break their bunk-timers and let them sleep on—or open their doors and watch them spoil.'

"So they agreed to do it," finished Moore, "and here we are, the last people alive on Earth, cavorting before machines operated by inhuman creatures who are watching us for incomprehensible reasons."

"Then we'll give them a good show," she replied, "and maybe they'll applaud us once before we spoil."

She snubbed out her cigar and kissed him good night. They returned to their refrigerators.

It was twelve weeks before Moore felt the need for a rest from the Party circuit. He was beginning to grow fearful. Leota had spent nonfunctional decades of her time vacationing with him, and she had recently been showing signs of sullenness, apparently regretting these expenditures on his behalf. So he decided to see something real, to take a stroll in the year 2078. After all, he was over a hundred years old.

The Queen Will Live Forever, said the faded clipping that

hung in the main corridor of the Hall of sleep. Beneath the
bannerline was the old/recent story of the conquest of the
final remaining problems of Multiple Sclerosis, and the medical ransom of one of its most notable victims. Moore had
not seen the Doyenne since the day of his interview. He did
not care whether he ever saw her again.

He donned a suit from his casualwear style locker and
strolled through the gardens and out to the airfield. There
were no people about.

He did not really know where he wanted to go until he
stood before a ticket booth and the speaker asked him, "Destination, please."

"Uh—Oahu. Akwa Labs, if they have a landing field of
their own."

"Yes, they do. That will have to be a private charter
though, for the final fifty-six miles—"

"Give me a private charter all the way, both ways."

"Insert your card, please."

He did.

After five seconds the card popped back into his waiting
hand. He dropped it into his pocket.

"What time will I arrive?" he asked.

"Nine hundred thirty-two, if you leave on Dart Nine six
minutes from now. Have you any luggage?"

"No."

"In that case, your Dart awaits you in area A-11."

Moore crossed the field to the VTO Dart numbered
"Nine." It flew by tape. The flight pattern, since it was a
specially chartered run, had been worked out back at the
booth, within milliseconds of Moore's naming his destination. It was then broadcast-transferred to a blank tape inside
Dart Nine; an auto-alternation brain permitted the Dart to
correct its course in the face of unforeseen contingencies and
later recorrect itself, landing precisely where it was sched-
uled to come down.

Moore mounted the ramp and stopped to slip his car into
the slot beside the hatchway. The hatch swung open and he
collected his card and entered. He selected a seat beside a
port and snapped its belt about his middle. At this, the hatchway swung itself shut.

After a few minutes the belt unfastened itself and vanished into the arms of his seat. The Dart was cruising smoothly now.

"Do you wish to have the lights dimmed? Or would you prefer to have them brighter?" asked a voice at his side.

"They're fine just the way they are," he told the invisible entity.

"Would you care for something to eat? Or something to drink?"

"I'll have a Martini."

There was a sliding sound, followed by a muted click. A tiny compartment opened in the wall beside him. His Martini rested within.

He removed it and sipped a sip.

Beyond the port and toward the rear of the Dart, a faint blue nimbus arose from the sideplates.

"Would you care for anything else?" *Pause.* "Shall I read you an article on the subject of your choice?" *Pause.* "Or fiction?" *Pause.* "Or poetry?" *Pause.* "Would you care to view the catalog?" *Pause.* "Or perhaps you would prefer music?"

"Poetry?" repeated Moore.

"Yes, I have many of—"

"I know a poet," he remembered. "Have you anything by Wayne Unger?"

There followed a brief mechanical meditation, then:

"Wayne Unger. Yes," answered the voice. "On call are his *Paradise Unwanted*, *Fungi of Steel*, and *Chisel in the Sky*."

"Which is his most recent work?" asked Moore.

"Chisel in the Sky."

"Read it to me."

The voice began by reading him all the publishing data and copyright information. To Moore's protests it answered that it was a matter of law and cited a precedent case. Moore asked for another Martini and waited.

Finally, " 'Our Wintered Way through Evening, and Burning Bushes Along It,' " said the voice.

"Huh?"

"That is the title of the first poem."

"Oh, read on."

" '(Where only the evergreens whiten . . .)

Winterflaked ashes heighten
in towers of blizzard.
Silhouettes unseal an outline.
Darkness, like an absence of faces,
pours from the opened home;
it seeps through shattered pine
and flows the fractured maple.

Perhaps it is the essence senescent,
dreamculled from the sleepers,
that soaks upon this road
in weather-born excess.
Or perhaps the great Anti-Life
learns to paint with a vengeance,
to run an icicle down the gargoyle's eye.

For properly speaking, though
no one can confront himself in toto,
I see your falling sky, gone gods,
as in a smoke-filled dream
of ancient statues burning,
soundlessly, down to the ground.

(. . . and never the everwhite's green.)' "

There was a ten-second pause, then: "The next poem is
entitled—"

"Wait a minute," asked Moore. "That first one—? Are
you programmed to explain anything about it?"

"I am sorry, I am not. That would require a more complicated unit."

"Repeat the copyright date of the book."

"2016, in the North American Union—"

"And it's his most recent work?"

"Yes, he is a member of Party Set and there is generally
a lapse of several decades between his books."

"Continue reading."

The machine read on. Moore knew little concerning verse,

but he was struck by the continual references to ice and cold, to snow and sleep.

"Stop," he told the machine. "Have you anything of his from before he joined the Set?"

"*Paradise Unwanted* was published in 1981, two years after he became a member. According to its Foreword, however, most of it was written prior to his joining."

"Read it."

Moore listened carefully. It contained little of ice, snow, or sleep. He shrugged at this minor discovery. His seat immediately adjusted and readjusted to the movement.

He barely knew Unger. He did not like his poetry. He did not like most poetry, though.

The reader began another.

" *'In the Dogged House,'* " it said.

" *'The heart is a graveyard of crigas,*
hid far from the hunter's eye,
where love wears death like enamel
and dogs crawl in to die . . .' "

Moore smiled as it read the other stanzas. Recognizing its source, he liked that one somewhat better.

"Stop reading," he told the machine.

He ordered a light meal and thought about Unger. He had spoken with him once. When was it?

2017 . . . ? Yes, at the Free Workers' Liberation Centennial in the Lenin Palace.

It was rivers of vodka. . . .

Fountains of juices, like inhuman arteries slashed, spurted their bright umbrellas of purple and lemon and green and orange. Jewels to ransom an Emir flashed near many hearts. Their host, Premier Korlov, seemed a happy frost giant in his display.

. . . In a dance pavilion of polaroid crystal, with the world outside blinking off and on, on and off—like an advertisement, Unger had commented, both elbows resting on the bartop and his foot on the indispensable rail.

His head had swiveled as Moore approached. He was a

bleary-eyed albino owl. "Albion Moore, I believe," he had said, extending a hand. "Quo vadis dammit?"

"Grape juice and wadka," said Moore to the unnecessary human standing beside the mix-machine. The uniformed man pressed two buttons and passed the glass across the two feet of frosty mahogany. Moore twitched it toward Unger in a small salute. "A happy Free Workers' Liberation Centennial to you."

"I'll drink to liberation." The poet leaned forward and poked his own combination of buttons. The man in the uniform sniffed audibly.

They drank a drink together.

"They accuse us"—Unger's gesture indicated the world at large—"of neither knowing nor caring anything about un-Set things, un-Set people."

"Well, it's true, isn't it?"

"Oh yes, but it might be expanded upon. We're the same way with our fellows. Be honest now, how many Setmen are you acquainted with?"

"Quite a few."

"I didn't ask how many names you knew."

"Well, I talk with them all the time. Our environment is suited to much movement and many words—and we have all the time in the world. How many friends do *you* have?" he asked.

"I just finished one," grunted the poet, leaning forward. "I'm going to mix me another."

Moore didn't feel like being depressed or joked with and he was not sure which category this fell into. He had been living inside a soap bubble since after the ill-starred Davy Jones Party, and he did not want anyone poking sharp things in his direction.

"So, you're your own man. If you're not happy in the Set, leave."

"You're not being a true *tovarisch*," said Unger, shaking a finger. "There was a time when a man could tell his troubles to bartenders and barfriends. You wouldn't remember, though—those days went out when the nickelplated barmatics came in. Damn their exotic eyes and scientific mixing!"

Suddenly he punched out three drinks in rapid succession. He slopped them across the dark, shiny surface.

"Taste them! Sip each of them!" he enjoined Moore. "Can't tell them apart without a scorecard, can you?"

"They're dependable that way."

"Dependable? Hell yes! Depend on them to create neurotics. One time a man could buy a beer and bend an ear. All that went out when the dependable mix-machines came in. Now we join a talk-out club of manic change and most unnatural! Oh, had the Mermaid been such!" he complained in false notes of frenzy. "Or the Bloody Lion of Stepney! What jaded jakes the fellows of Marlowe had been!"

He sagged.

"Aye! Drinking's not what it used to be."

The international language of his belch caused the mix-machine attendant to avert his face, which betrayed a pained expression before he did so.

"So I'll repeat my question," stated Moore, making conversation. "Why do you stay where you're unhappy? You could go open a real bar of your own, if that's what you'd like. It would probably be a success, now that I think of it—people serving drinks and all that."

"Go to! Go to! I shan't say where!" He stared at nothing. "Maybe that's what I'll do someday, though," he reflected, "open a real bar. . . ."

Moore turned his back to him then, to watch Leota dancing with Korlov. He was happy.

"People join the Set for a variety of reasons," Unger was muttering, "but the main one is exhibitionism, with the titillating wraith of immortality lurking at the stage door, perhaps. Attracting attention to oneself gets harder and harder as time goes one. It's almost impossible in the sciences. In the nineteenth and twentieth centuries you could still name great names—now it's great research teams. The arts have been democratized out of existence—and where have all the audiences gone? I don't mean spectators either.

"So we have the Set," he continued. "Take our sleeping beauty there, dancing with Korlov—"

"Huh?"

"Pardon me, I didn't mean to awaken you abruptly. I was

saying that if she wanted attention Miss Mason couldn't be a
stripper today, so she had to join the Set. It's even better than
being a threelie star, and it requires less work—''

''Stripper?''

''A folk artist who undressed to music.''

''Yes, I recall hearing of them.''

''That's gone too, though,'' sighed Unger, ''and while I
cannot disapprove of the present customs of dress and un-
dress, it still seems to me as if something bright and frail
died in the elder world.''

''She *is* bright, isn't she?''

''Decidedly so.''

They had taken a short walk then, outside, in the cold night
of Moscow. Moore did not really want to leave, but he had
had enough to drink so that he was easy to persuade. Besides
that, he did not want the stumbling babbler at his side to fall
into an excavation or wander off lost, to miss his flight or
turn up injured. So they shuffled up bright avenues and down
dim streets until they came to the Square. They stopped before a large, dilapidated monument. The poet broke a small
limb from a shrub and bent it into a wreath. He tossed it
against the wall.

''Poor fellow,'' he muttered.

''Who?''

''The guy inside.''

''Who's that?''

Unger cocked his head at him.

''You really don't know?''

''I admit there are gaps in my education, if that's what you
mean. I continually strive to fill them, but I always was weak
on history. I specialized at an early age.''

Unger jerked his thumb at the monument.

''Noble Macbeth lies in state within,'' he said. ''He was
an ancient king who slew his predecessor, noble Duncan,
most heinously. Lots of other people too. When he took the
throne he promised he'd be nice to his subjects, though. But
the Slavic temperament is a strange thing. He is best remembered for his many fine speeches, which were translated by
a man named Pasternak. Nobody reads them anymore.''

Unger sighed and seated himself on a stair. Moore joined

him. He was too cold to be insulted by the arrogant mocking of the drunken poet.

"Back then, people used to fight wars," said Unger.

"I know," responded Moore, his fingers freezing; "Napoleon once burnt part of this city."

Unger tipped his hat.

Moore scanned the skyline. A bewildering range of structures hedged the Square—here, bright and functional, a ladder-like office building composed its heights and witnessed distances, as only the planned vantages of the very new can manage; there, a daytime aquarium of an agency was now a dark mirror, a place where the confidence-inspiring efficiencies of rehearsed officials were displayed before the onlooker; and across the Square, its purged youth fully restored by shadow, a deserted onion of a cupola poked its sharp topknot after soaring vehicles, a number of which, scuttling among the star fires, were indicated even now—and Moore blew upon his fingers and jammed his hands into his pockets.

"Yes, nations went to war," Unger was saying. "Artilleries thundered. Blood was spilled. People died. But we lived through it, crossing a shaky Shinvat word by word. Then one day there it was. Peace. It had been that way a long time before anyone noticed. We still don't know how we did it. Perpetual postponement and a short memory, I guess, as man's attention became occupied twenty-four hours a day with other things. Now there is nothing left to fight over, and everyone is showing off the fruits of peace—because everyone has some, by the roomful. All they want. More. These things that fill the rooms, though," he mused, "and the mind—how they have proliferated! Each month's version is better than the last, in some hypersophisticated manner. They seem to have absorbed the minds that are absorbed with them. . . ."

"We could all go live in the woods," said Moore, wishing he had taken the time to pocket a battery crystal and a thermostat for his suit.

"We could do lots of things, and we will, eventually—I suppose. Still, I guess we *could* wind up in the woods, at that."

"In that case, let's go back to the Palace while there's still time. I'm frozen."

"Why not?"

They climbed to their feet, began walking back.

"Why *did* you join the Set anyhow? So you could be discontent over the centuries?"

"Nay, son," the poet clapped him on the shoulder. "I'm an audience in search of an entertainment."

It took Moore an hour to get the chill out of his bones.

"Ahem. Ahem," said the voice. "We are about to land at Akwa Labs, Oahu."

The belt snaked out into Moore's lap. He snapped it tight.

A sudden feeling prompted him to ask: "Read me that last poem from *Chisel* again."

" '*Future Be Not Impatient*,' " stated the voice:

> " '*Someday, perhaps, but not this day.*
> *Sometime; but then, not now.*
> *Man is a monument-making mammal.*
> *Never ask me how.*' "

He thought of Leota's description of the moon and he hated Unger for the forty-four seconds it took him to disembark. He was not certain why.

He stood beside Dart Nine and watched the approach of a small man wearing a smile and gay tropical clothing. He shook hands automatically.

". . . Very pleased," the man named Teng was saying, "and glad there's not much around for you to recognize anymore. We've been deciding what to show you ever since Bermuda called." Moore pretended to be aware of the call. ". . . Not many people remember their employers from as far back as you do," Teng was saying.

Moore smiled and fell into step with him, heading toward the Processing Complex.

"Yes, I was curious," he agreed, "to see what it all looks like now. My old office, my lab—"

"Gone, of course."

". . . our first chamber-tandem, with its big-nozzled in-
jectors—"

"Replaced, naturally."

"Naturally. And the big old pumps . . ."

"Shiny and new."

Moore brightened. The sun, which he had not seen for
several days/years, felt good on his back, but the air conditioning felt even better as they entered the first building. There
was something of beauty in the pure functional compactness
of everything about them, something Unger might have called
by a different name, he realized, but it was beauty to Moore.
He ran his hand along the sides of the units he did not have
time to study. He tapped the conduits and peered into the
kilns which processed the by-product ceramicware; he nodded approval and paused to relight his pipe whenever the man
at his side asked his opinion of something too technically
remote for him to have any opinion.

They crossed catwalks, moved through the temple-like in-
nards of shut-down tanks, traversed alley-ways where the silent, blinking panels indicated that unseen operations were
in progress. Occasionally they met a worker, seated before a
sleeping trouble-board, watching a broadcast entertainment
or reading something over his portable threelie. Moore shook
hands and forgot names.

Processing Director Teng could not help but be partly hyp-
notized—both by Moore's youthful appearance and by the
knowledge that he had developed a key process at some past
date (as well as by his apparent understanding of present
operations)—into believing that he was an engineer of his
own breed, and up-to-date in his education. Actually, Mary
Mullen's prediction that his profession would some day move
beyond the range of his comprehension had not yet come to
pass—but he could see that it was the direction in which he
was headed. Appropriately, he had noticed his photo gathering dust in a small lobby, amid those of Teng's other dead
and retired predecessors.

Sensing this feeling, Moore asked, "Say, do you think I
could have my old job back?"

The man's head jerked about. Moore remained expression-
less.

"Well—I suppose—something—could be worked . . ." he ended lamely as Moore broke into a grin and twisted the question back into casual conversation. It was somehow amusing to have produced that sudden, strange look of realization on the man's bored face, as he actually *saw* Moore for the first time. Frightening, too.

"Yes, seeing all this progress—is inspiring," Moore pronounced, "It's almost enough to make a man want to work again. —Glad I don't have to, of course. But there's a bit of nostalgia involved in coming back after all these years and seeing how this place grew out of the shoestring operation it seemed then—grew into more buildings than I could walk through in a week, and all of them packed with new hardware and working away to beat the band. Smooth. Efficient. I like it. I suppose you like working here?"

"Yes," sighed Teng, "as much as a man can like working. Say, were you planning on staying overnight? There's a weekly employees' luau and you'd be very welcome." He glanced at the wafer of a watchface clinging to his wrist. "In fact, it's already started," he added.

"Thanks," said Moore, "but I have a date and I have to be going. I just wanted to reaffirm my faith in progress. Thanks for the tour, and thanks for your time."

"Any time." Teng steered him toward a lush Break Room. "You won't be wanting to Dart back for awhile yet, will you?" he said. "So while we're having a bite to eat in here I wonder if I could ask you some questions about the Set. Its entrance requirements in particular. . . ."

All the way around the world to Bermuda, getting happily drunk in the belly of Dart Nine, in the year of Our Lord twenty seventy-eight, Moore felt that Time had been put aright.

"So you want to have it./?" said/asked Mary Maude, uncoiling carefully from the caverns of her shawl.

"Yes."

"Why?" she asked.

"Because I do not destroy that which belongs to me. I possess so very little as it is."

The Doyenne snorted gently, perhaps in amusement. She tapped her favorite dog, as though seeking a reply from it.

"Though it sails upon a bottomless sea toward some fabulous orient," she mused, "the ship will still attempt to lower an anchor. I do not know why. Can you tell me? Is it simply carelessness on the part of the captain? Or the second mate?"

The dog did not answer. Neither did anything else.

"Or is it a mutineer's desire to turn around and go back?" she inquired. "To return home?"

There was a brief stillness. Finally:

"I live in a succession of homes. They are called hours. Each is lovely."

"But not lovely enough, and never to be revisited, eh? Permit me to anticipate your next words: 'I do not intend to marry. I do not intend to leave the Set. I shall have my child—' By the way, what will it be, a boy or a girl?"

"A girl."

" '—I shall have my daughter. I shall place her in a fine home, arrange her a glorious future, and be back in time for the Spring Festival.' " She rubbed her glazed dog as though it were a crystal and pretended to peer through its greenish opacity. "Am I not a veritable gypsy?" she asked.

"Indeed."

"And you think this will work out?"

"I fail to see why it should not."

"Tell me which her proud father will do," she inquired, "compose her a sonnet sequence, or design her mechanical toys?"

"Neither. He shall never know. He'll be asleep until spring, and I will not. *She* must never know either."

"So much the worse."

"Why, pray tell?"

"Because she will become a woman in less than two months, by the clock of the Set—and a lovely woman, I daresay—because she will be able to afford loveliness."

"Of course."

"And, as the daughter of a member, she will be eminently eligible for Set candidacy."

"She may not want it."

"Only those who cannot achieve it allude to having those

sentiments. No, she'll want it. Everyone does. —And, if her beauty should be surgically obtained, I believe that I shall, in this instance, alter a rule of mine. I shall pass on her and admit her to the Set. She will then meet many interesting people—poets, engineers, her mother. . . ."

"No! I'd tell her, before I'd permit that to happen!"

"Aha! Tell me, is your fear of incest predicated upon your fear of competition, or is it really the other way around?"

"Please! Why are you saying these horrible things?"

"Because, unfortunately, you are something I can no longer afford to keep around. You have been an excellent symbol for a long time, but now your pleasures have ceased to be Olympian. Yours is a lapse into the mundane. You show that the gods are less sophisticated than schoolchildren—that they can be victimized by biology, despite the oceans of medical allies at our command. Princess, in the eyes of the world you are my daughter, for I am the Set. So take some motherly advice and retire. Do not attempt to renew your option. Get married first, and then go to sleep for a few months—till spring, when your option is up. Sleep intermittently in the bunker, so that a year or so will pass. We'll play up the romantic aspects of your retirement. Wait a year or two to bear your child. The cold sleep won't do her any harm; there have been other cases such as yours. If you fail to agree to this, our motherly ad-monition is that you face present expulsion."

"You *can't*!"

"Read your contract."

"But no one need ever know!"

"You silly little dollface!" The acetylene blazed forth. "Your glimpses of the outside have been fragmentary and extremely selective—for at least sixty years. Every news medium in the world watches almost every move every Setman makes, from the time he sits up in his bunker until he retires, exhausted, after the latest Party. Snoopers and newshounds today have more gimmicks and gadgets in their arsenals than your head has colorful hairs. We *can't* hide your daughter all her life, so we won't even try. We'd have trouble enough concealing matters if you decided not to have her—but I think we could outbribe and outdrug our own employees.

"Therefore, I call upon you for a decision."

"I am sorry."

"So am I," said the Doyenne.

The girl stood.

From somewhere, as she left, she seemed to hear the whimpering of a china dog.

Beyond the neat hedgerows of the garden and down a purposefully irregular slope ran the unpaved pathway that wandered, like an impulsive river, through neck-tickling straits of unkempt forsythia, past high islands of mobbed sumac, and by the shivering branches, like waves, of an occasional ginkgo, wagging at the overhead gulls, while dreaming of the high-flying Archaeopteryx about to break through its heart in a dive; and perhaps a thousand feet of twistings are required to negotiate the two hundred feet of planned wilderness that separates the gardens of the Hall of Sleep from the artificial ruins which occupy a full, hilly acre, dotted here and there by incipient jungles of lilac and the occasional bell of a great willow—which momentarily conceal, and then guide the eye on toward broken pediments, smashed friezes, half-standing, shred-topped columns, then fallen columns, then faceless, handless statues, and finally, seemingly random heaps of rubble which lay amid these things; here, the path over which they moved then forms a delta and promptly loses itself where the tides of Time chafe away the memento mori quality that the ruins first seem to spell, acting as a temporal entasis and in the eye of the beholding Setman, so that he can look upon it all and say, "I am older than this," and his companion can reply, "We will pass again some year and this, too, will be gone," (even though she did not say it this time) feeling happier by feeling the less mortal by so doing; and crossing through the rubble, as they did, to a place where barbarously ruined Pan grins from inside the ring of a dry fountain, a new path is to be located, this time an unplanned and only recently formed way, where the grass is yellowed underfoot and the walkers must go single file because it leads them through a place of briars, until they reach the old breakwall over which they generally climb like commandos in order to gain access to a quarter-mile strand of coved and deserted beach, where the sand is not quite so clean as the beaches of the town—which are generally sifted every third day—but where the shade is as intense, in its own way, as the sunlight, and there are flat rocks offshore for meditation.

"You're getting lazy," he commented, kicking off his shoes and digging his toes into the cool sand. "You didn't climb over."

"I'm getting lazy," she agreed.

They threw off their robes and walked to the water's edge.

"Don't push!"

"Come on. I'll race you to the rocks."

For once he won.

Loafing in the lap of the Atlantic, they could have been any two bathers in any place, in any time.

"I could stay here forever."

"It gets cold nights, and if there's a bad storm you might catch something or get washed away."

"I meant," she amended, "if it could always be like this."

" 'Verweile doch, du bist so schön,' " he reminded. "Faust lost a bet that way, remember? So would a Sleeper. Unger's got me reading again—Hey! What's the matter?"

"Nothing!"

"There's something wrong, little girl. Even I can tell."

"So what if there is?"

"So a lot, that's what. Tell me."

Her hand bridged the narrow channel between their rocks and found his. He rolled onto his side and stared at her satin-wet hair and her stuck-together eyelashes, the dimpled deserts of her cheeks, and the bloodied oasis of her mouth. She squeezed his hand.

"Let's stay here forever—despite the chill, and being washed away."

"You are indicating that—?"

"We could get off at this stop."

"I suppose. But—"

"But you like it now? You like the big charade?"

He looked away.

"I think you were right," she told him, "that night—many years ago."

"What night?"

"The night you said it was all a joke—that we are the last

people alive on Earth, performing before machines operated by inhuman creatures who watch us for incomprehensible purposes. What are we but wave-patterns on an oscilloscope? I'm sick of being an object of contemplation!''

He continued to stare into the sea.

''I'm rather fond of the Set now,'' he finally responded. ''At first I was ambivalent toward it. But a few weeks—years—ago I visited a place where I used to work. It was—different. Bigger. Better run. But more than that actually. It wasn't just that it was filled with things I couldn't have guessed at fifty or sixty years ago. I had an odd feeling while I was there. I was with a little chatterbox of a Processing Director named Teng, and he was yammering away worse than Unger, and I was just staring at all those tandem-tanks and tiers of machinery that had grown up inside the shell of that first old building—sort of like inside a womb—and I suddenly felt that someday something was going to be born, born of steel and plastic and dancing electrons, in such a stainless, sunless place—and *that* something would be so fine that I would want to be there to see it. I couldn't dignify it by calling it a mystical experience or anything like that. It was just sort of a feeling I had. But if *that* moment could stay forever . . . Anyhow, the Set is my ticket to a performance I'd like to see.''

''Darling,'' she began, ''it is anticipation and recollection that fill the heart—never the sensation of the moment.''

''Perhaps you are right. . . .''

His grip tightened on her hand as the tunnel between their eyes shortened. He leaned across the water and kissed the blood from her mouth.

''Verweile doch . . . ''

''. . . Du bist so schön.''

It was the Party to end all Parties. The surprise announcement of Alvin Moore and Leota Mathilde Mason struck the Christmas Eve gathering of the Set as just the thing for the season. After an extensive dinner and the exchange of bright and costly trifles the lights were dimmed. The giant Christmas tree atop the transparent penthouse blazed like a compressed galaxy through the droplets of melted snow on the ceilingpane.

It was nine by all the clocks of London.

"Married on Christmas, divorced on Twelfth Night," said someone in the darkness.

"What'll they do for an encore?" whispered someone else.

There were giggles and several off-key carols followed them. The backlight pickup was doubtless in action.

"Tonight we are quaint," said Moore.

"We danced in Davy Jones' Locker," answered Leota, "while they cringed and were sick on the floor."

"It's not the same Set," he told her, "not really. How many new faces have you counted? How many old ones have vanished? It's hard to tell. Where do old Setman go?"

"The graveyard of the elephants?" she suggested. "Who knows?"

" *'The heart is a graveyard of crigas,'* " recited Moore,
" *'hid far from the hunter's eye,*
where love wears death like enamel
and dogs crawl in to die.' "

"That's Unger's, isn't it?" she asked.

"That's right, I just happened to recall it."

"I wish you hadn't. I don't like it."

"Sorry."

"Where is Unger anyway?" she asked as the darkness retreated and the people arose.

"Probably at the punchbowl—or under the table."

"Not this early in the evening—for being under the table, I mean."

Moore shifted.

"What *are* we doing here anyhow?" he wanted to know. "Why did we have to attend this Party?"

"Because it is the season of charity."

"Faith and hope, too," he smirked. "You want to be maudlin or something? All right, I'll be maudlin with you. It *is* a pleasure, really."

He raised her hand to his lips.

"Stop that!"

"All right."

He kissed her on the mouth. There was laughter.

She flushed but did not rise from his side.

"If you want to make a fool of me—of us," he said, "I'll go more than halfway. Tell me why we had to come to this Party and announce our un-Setness before everyone? We could have just faded away from the Parties, slept until spring, and let our options run out."

"No. I am a woman and I could not resist another Party— the last one of the year, the very last—and wear your gift on my finger and know that deep down inside, the others *do* envy us—our courage, if nothing else—and probably our happiness."

"Okay," he agreed, "I'll drink to it—to you, anyway." He raised his glass and downed it. There was no fireplace to throw it into, so as much as he admired the gesture he placed it back on the table.

"Shall we dance? I hear music."

"Not yet. Let's just sit here and drink."

"Fine."

When all the clocks in London said eleven, Leota wanted to know where Unger was.

"He left," a slim girl with purple hair told her, "right after dinner. Maybe indigestion"—she shrugged—"or maybe he went looking for the Globe."

She frowned and took another drink.

Then they danced. Moore did not really see the room through which they moved, nor the other dancers. They were all the featureless characters in a book he had already closed. Only the dance was real—and the woman with whom he was dancing.

Time's friction, he decided, and a raising of the sights. I have what I wanted and still I want more. I'll get over it.

It was a vasty hall of mirrors. There were hundreds of Alvin Moores and Leotas (née Mason) dancing. They were dancing at all their Parties of the past seventy-some years— from a Tibetan ski lodge to Davy Jones' Locker, from a New Year's Eve in orbit to the floating Palace of Kanayasha, from a Halloween in the caverns of Carlsbad to a Mayday at Delphi—they had danced everywhere, and tonight was the last Party, *good night, ladies*. . . .

She leaned against him and said nothing and her breath collared his neck.

"Good night, good night, good night," he heard himself saying, and they left with the bells of midnight, early, early, and it was Christmas as they entered the hopcar and told the Set chauffeur that they were returning early.

And they passed over the stratocruiser and settled beside the Dart they had come in, and they crossed through the powdery fleece that lay on the ground and entered the smaller craft.

"Do you wish to have the lights dimmed? Or would you prefer to have them brighter?" asked a voice at their side, after London and its clocks and its Bridge had fallen, down.

"Dim them."

"Would you care for something to eat? Or something to drink?"

"No."

"No."

"Shall I read you an article on the subject of your choice?" *Pause*. "Or fiction?" *Pause*. "Or poetry?" *Pause*. "Would you care to view the catalog?" *Pause*. "Or perhaps you would prefer music?"

"Music," she said. "Soft. Not the kind you listen to."

After about ten minutes of near-sleep, Moore heard the voice:

> *"Hilted of flame,*
> *our frail phylactic blade*
> *slits black*
> *beneath Polestar's*
> *pinprick comment,*
> *foredging burrs*
> *of mitigated hell,*
> *spilling light without illumination.*
>
> *Strands of song,*
> *to share its stinging flight,*
> *are shucked and scraped*

> to fit an idiot theme.
> Here, through outlocked chaos,
> climbed of migrant logic,
> the forms of black notation
> blackly dice a flame.''

"Turn it off," said Moore. "We didn't ask you to read."

"I'm not reading," said the voice, "I'm composing."

"Who—?"

Moore came awake and turned in his seat, which promptly adjusted to the movement. A pair of feet projected over the arm of a double seat to the rear.

"Unger?"

"No, Santa Claus. Ho! Ho!"

"What are you doing going back this early?"

"You just answered your own question, didn't you?"

Moore snorted and settled back once more. At his side, Leota was snoring delicately, her seat collapsed into a couch.

He shut his eyes, but knowing they were not alone he could not regain the peaceful drifting sensation he had formerly achieved. He heard a sigh and the approach of lurching footfalls. He kept his eyes closed, hoping Unger would fall over and go to sleep. He didn't.

Abruptly, his voice rang out, a magnificently dreadful baritone:

"I was down to Saint James's Infir-r-rmary," he sang. "I saw my ba-a-aby there, stretched out on a long whi-i-ite ta-a-able—so sweet, so cold, so fair—"

Moore swung his left hand, cross-body at the poet's midsection. He had plenty of target, but he was too slow. Unger blocked his fist and backed away, laughing.

Leota shook herself awake.

"What are you doing here?" she asked.

"Composing," he answered, "myself."

"Merry Christmas," he added.

"Go to hell," answered Moore.

"I congratulate you on your recent nuptials, Mister Moore."

"Thanks."

"Why wasn't I invited?"

"It was a simple ceremony."

He turned.

"Is that true, Leota? An old comrade in arms like me, not invited just because it wasn't showy enough for my elaborate tastes?"

She nodded, fully awake now.

He struck his forehead.

"Oh, I am wounded!"

"Why don't you go back to wherever you came from?" asked Moore. "The drinks are on the house."

"I can't attend midnight mass in an inebriated condition."

Moore's fingers twitched back into fists.

"You may attend a mass for the dead without having to kneel."

"I believe you are hinting that you wish to be alone. I understand."

He withdrew to the rear of the Dart. After a time he began to snore.

"I hope we never see him again," she said.

"Why? He's a harmless drunk."

"No, he isn't. He hates us—because we're happy and he isn't."

"I think he's happiest when he's unhappy," smiled Moore, "and whenever the temperature drops. He loves the cold-bunk because it's like a little death to sleep in it. He once said, 'Each Setman dies many deaths. That's what I like about being a Setman.'"

"You say more sleep won't be injurious—" he asked abruptly.

"No, there's no risk."

Below them, Time fled backward through the cold. Christmas was pushed out into the hallway and over the threshold of the front door to their world—Alvin's, Leota's, and Unger's world—to stand shivering on the doorsill of its own Eve, in Bermuda.

Inside the Dart, passing backward through Time, Moore recalled that New Year's Eve Party many years ago, recalled his desires of that day and reflected that they sat beside him now; recalled the Parties since then and reflected that he would miss all that were yet to come; recalled his work in

the time before Time—a few months ago—and reflected that
he could no longer do it properly—and that Time was indeed
out of joint and that *he* could not set it aright; he recalled his
old apartment, never revisited, all his old friends, including
Diane Demetrios, now dead or senile, and reflected that, beyond the Set which he was leaving, he knew no one, save
possibly the girl at his side. Only Wayne Unger was ageless,
for he was an employee of the eternal. Given a month or two
Unger could open up a bar, form his own circle of outcasts
and toy with a private renaissance, if he should ever decide
to leave.

Moore suddenly felt very stale and tired, and he whispered
to their ghostly servant for a Martini and reached across his
dozing wife to fetch it from the cubicle. He sat there sipping
it, wondering about the world below.

He should have kept with life, he decided. He knew nothing of contemporary politics, or law, or art; his standards
were those grafted on by the Set, and concerned primarily
with color, movement, gaiety, and clever speech; he was re-
duced again to childhood when it came to science. He knew
he was wealthy, but the Set had been managing all his finances. All he had was an all-purpose card, good anywhere
in the world for any sort of purchase, commodity- or service-
wise. Periodically, he had examined his file and seen balance
sheets which told him he need never worry about being short
of money. But he did not feel confident or competent when
it came to meeting the people who resided in the world outside. Perhaps he would appear stodgy, old-fashioned, and
"quaint" as he had felt tonight, without the glamor of the
Set to mask his humanity.

Unger snored. Leota breathed deeply, and the world turned.
When they reached Bermuda they returned to the Earth.

They stood beside the Dart, just outside the flight terminal.

"Care to take a walk?" asked Moore.

"I am tired, my love," said Leota, staring in the direction
of the Hall of Sleep. She looked back.

He shook his head. "I'm not quite ready."

She returned to him. He kissed her.

"I'll see you then in April, darling. Good night."

"April is the cruelest month," observed Unger. "Come, engineer. I'll walk with you are far as the shuttle stands."

They began walking. They moved across the roadway in the direction opposite the terminal, and they entered upon the broad, canopied walk that led to the ro-car garage.

It was a crystalline night, with stars like tinsel and a satellite beacon blazing like a gold piece deep within the pool of the sky. As they walked, their breath fumed into white wreaths that vanished before they were fully formed. Moore tried in vain to light his pipe. Finally, he stopped and hunched his shoulders against the wind until he got it going.

"A good night for walking," said Unger.

Moore grunted. A gust of wind lashed a fiery rain of loose tobacco upon his cheek. He smoked on, hands in the pockets of his jacket, collar raised. The poet clapped him on the shoulder.

"Come with me into the town," he suggested. "It's only over the hill. We can walk it."

"No," said Moore, through his teeth.

They strode on, and as they neared the garage Unger grew uneasy.

"I'd rather someone were with me tonight," he said abruptly. "I feel strange, as though I'd drunk the draught of the centuries and suddenly am wise in a time when wisdom is unnecessary. I—I'm afraid."

Moore hesitated.

"No," he finally repeated. "it's time to say good-bye. You're traveling on and we're getting off. Have fun."

Neither offered to shake hands, and Moore watched him move into the shuttle stop.

Continuing behind the building, Moore cut diagonally across the wide lawns and into the garden. He strolled aimlessly for a few minutes, then found the path that led down to the ruins.

The going was slow and he wound his way through the cold wilderness. After a period of near-panic when he felt surrounded by trees and had to backtrack, he emerged into the starlit clearing where menaces of shrubbery dappled the broken buildings with patterns of darkness, moving restlessly as the winds shifted.

The grass rustled about his ankles as he seated himself on a fallen pillar and got his pipe going once more.

He sat thinking himself into marble as his toes grew numb, and he felt very much a part of the place; an artificial scene, a ruin transplanted out of history onto unfamiliar grounds. He did not want to move. He just wanted to freeze into the landscape and become his own monument. He sat there making pacts with imaginary devils: he wanted to go back, to return with Leota to his Frisco town, to work again. Like Unger, he suddenly felt wise in time when wisdom was unnecessary. Knowledge was what he needed. Fear was what he had.

Pushed on by the wind, he picked his way across the plain. Within the circle of his fountain, Pan was either dead or sleeping. Perhaps it is the cold sleep of the gods, decided Moore, and Pan will one day awaken and blow upon his festival pipes and only the wind among high towers will answer, and the shuffling tread of an assessment robot be quickened to scan him—because the Party people will have forgotten the festival melodies, and the waxen ones will have isolated out the wisdom of the blood on their colored slides and inoculated mankind against it—and programmed against emotions, a frivolity machine will perpetually generate the sensations of gaiety into the fever-dreams of the delirious, so that they will not recognize his tunes—and there shall be none among the children of Phoebus to even repeat the Attic cry of his first passing, heard those many Christmases ago beyond the waters of the Mediterranean.

Moore wished that he had stayed a little longer with Unger, because he now felt that he had gained a glimpse of the man's perspective. It had taken the fear of a new world to generate these feelings, but he was beginning to understand the poet. Why did the man stay on in the Set, though? he wondered. Did he take a masochistic pleasure in seeing his ice-prophecies fulfilled, as he moved further and further away from his own times? Maybe that was it.

Moore stirred himself into one last pilgrimage. He walked along their old path down to the breakwall. The stones were cold beneath his fingers, so he used the stile to cross over to the beach.

He stood on a rim of rust at the star-reflecting bucket-bottom of the world. He stared out at the black humps of the rocks where they had held their sunny colloquy days/months ago. It was his machines he had spoken of then, before they had spoken of themselves. He had believed, still believed, in their inevitable fusion with the spirit of his kind, into greater and finer vessels for life. Now he feared, like Unger, that by the time this occurred something else might have been lost, and that the fine new vessels would only be partly filled, lacking some essential ingredient. He hoped Unger was wrong; he felt that the ups and downs of Time might at some future equinox restore all those drowsing verities of the soul's undersides that he was now feeling—and that there *would* be ears to hear the piped melody, and feet that would move with its sound. He tried to believe this. He hoped it would be true.

A star fell, and Moore looked at his watch. It was late. He scuffed his way back to the wall and crossed over it again.

Inside the pre-sleep clinic he met Jameson, who was already yawning from his prep-injection. Jameson was a tall, thin man with the hair of a cherub and the eyes of its opposite number.

"Moore," he grinned, watching him hang his jacket on the wall and roll up his sleeve, "you going to spend your honeymoon on ice?"

The hypogun sighed in the medic's husky hand and the prep-injection entered Moore's arm.

"That's right," he replied, leveling his gaze at the not completely sober Jameson. "Why?"

"It just doesn't seem the thing to do," Jameson explained, still grinning. "If I were married to Leota you wouldn't catch me going on ice. Unless—"

Moore took one step toward him, the sound in his throat like a snarl. Jameson drew back, his dark eyes widening.

"I was joking!" he said. "I didn't . . . ."

There was a pain in Moore's injected arm as the big medic seized it and jerked him to a halt.

"Yeah," said Moore, "good night. Sleep tight, wake sober."

As he turned toward the door the medic released his arm.

Moore rolled down his sleeve and donned his jacket as he left.

"You're off your rocker," Jameson called after him.

Moore had about half an hour before he had to hit his bunker. He did not feel like heading for it at the moment. He had planned on waiting in the clinic until the injection began to work, but Jameson's presence changed that.

He walked through the wide corridors of the Hall of Sleep, rode a lift up to the bunkers, then strode down the hallway until he came to his door. He hesitated, then passed on. He would sleep there for the next three and a half months; he did not feel like giving it half of the next hour also.

He refilled his pipe. He would smoke through a sentinel watch beside the ice goddess, his wife. He looked about for wandering medics. One is supposed to refrain from smoking after the prep-injection, but it had never bothered him yet, or anyone else he knew of.

An intermittent thumping sound reached his ears as he moved on up the hallway. It stopped as he rounded a corner, then began again, louder. It was coming from up ahead.

After a moment there was another silence.

He paused outside Leota's door. Grinning around his pipe, he found a pen and drew a line through the last name on her plate. He printed "Moore" in above it. As he was forming the final letter the pounding began again.

It was coming from inside her room.

He opened the door, took a step, then stopped.

The man had his back to him. His right arm was raised. A mallet was clenched in his fist.

His panted mutterings, like an incantation, reached Moore's ears:

" 'Strew on her roses, roses, and never a spray of yew . . . In quiet she reposes—' "

Moore was across the chamber. He seized the mallet and managed to twist it away. Then he felt something break inside his hand as his first connected with a jaw. The man collided with the opposite wall, then pitched forward onto the floor.

"Leota!" said Moore. "Leota . . ."

Cast of white Parian she lay, deep within the coils of the bunker. The canopy had been raised high overhead. Her flesh

was already firm as stone—because there was no blood on
her breast where the stake had been driven in. Only cracks
and fissures, as in stone.

"No," said Moore.

The stake was a very hard synthowood—like cocobolo, or
quebracho, or perhaps lignum vitae—still to be unsplin-
tered. . . .

"No," said Moore.

Her face had the relaxed expression of a dreamer, her hair
was the color of aluminum. His ring was on her finger. . . .

There was a murmuring in the corner of the room.

"Unger," he said flatly, "why—did—you—do it?"

The man sucked air around his words. His eyes were focused on something nameless.

". . . Vampire," he muttered, "luring men aboard her
Flying Dutchman to drain them across the years. . . . She is
the future—a goddess on the outside and a thirsting vacuum
within," he stated without emotion. " 'Strew on her roses,
roses . . . Her mirth the world required—She bathed it in
smiles of glee . . .' She was going to leave me way up here
in the middle of the air. I can't get off the merry-go-round
and I can't have the brass ring. But no one else will lose as
I have lost, not now. '. . . Her life was turning, turning, in
mazes of heat and sound—' I thought she would come back
to me, after she'd tired of you."

He raised his hand to cover his eyes as Moore advanced
upon him.

"To the technician, the future—"

Moore hit him with the hammer, once, twice. After the
third blow he lost count because his mind could not conceive
of any number greater than three.

Then he was walking, running, the mallet still clutched in
his hand—past doors like blind eyes, up corridors, down
seldom-used stairwells.

As he lurched away from the Hall of Sleep he heard someone calling after him through the night. He kept running.

After a long while he began to walk again. His hand was
aching and his breath burned within his lungs. He climbed a
hill, paused at its top, then descended the other side.

Party Town, an expensive resort—owned and sponsored,

though seldom patronized by the Set—was deserted, except for the Christmas lights in the windows, and the tinsel, and the boughs of holly. From some dim adytum the recorded carols of a private celebration could be heard, and some laughter. These things made Moore feel even more alone as he walked up one street and down another, his body seeming ever more a thing apart from him as the prep-injection took its inevitable effect. His feet were leaden. His eyes kept closing and he kept forcing them back open.

There were no services going on when he entered the church. It was warmer inside. He was alone there, too.

The interior of the church was dim, and he was attracted to an array of lights about the display at the foot of a statue. It was a manger scene. He leaned back against a pew and stared at the mother and the child, at the angels and the inquisitive cattle, at the father. Then he made a sound he had no words for and threw the mallet into the little stable and turned away. Clawing at the wall, he staggered off a dozen steps and collapsed, cursing and weeping, until he slept.

They found him at the foot of the cross.

Justice had become a thing of streamlined swiftness since the days of Moore's boyhood. The sheer force of world population had long ago crowded every docket of every court to impossible extremes, until measures were taken to waive as much of the paraphernalia as could be waived and hold court around the clock. That was why Moore faced judgment at ten o'clock in the evening, two days after Christmas.

The trial lasted less than a quarter of an hour. Moore waived representation; the charges were read; he entered a plea of guilty, and the judge sentenced him to death in the gas chamber without looking up from the stack of papers on his bench.

Numbly, Moore left the courtroom and was returned to a cell for his final meal, which he did not remember eating. He had no conception of the juridical process in this year in which he had come to rest. The Set attorney had simply looked bored as he told him his story, then mentioned "symbolic penalties" and told him to waive representation and enter a simple plea of "guilty to the homicide as described."

He signed a statement to that effect. Then the attorney had left him and Moore had not spoken with anyone but his warders up until the time of the trial, and then only a few words before he went into court. And now—to receive a death sentence after he had admitted he was guilty of killing his wife's murderer—he could not conceive that justice had been done. Despite this, he felt an unnatural calm as he chewed mechanically upon whatever he had ordered. He was not afraid to die. He could not believe in it.

An hour later they came for him. He was led to a small, airtight room with a single, thick window set high in its metal door. He seated himself upon the bench within it and his gray-uniformed guards slammed the door behind him.

After an interminable time he heard the pellets breaking and he smelled the fumes. They grew stronger.

Finally, he was coughing and breathing fire and gasping and crying out, and he thought of her lying there in her bunker, the ironic strains of Unger's song during their Dart-flight recurring in his mind:

> *"I was down to Saint James' Infir-r-rmary.*
> *I saw my ba-a-aby there,*
> *Stretched out on a long whi-i-ite ta-a-able—*
> *So sweet, so cold, so fair . . ."*

Had Unger been consciously contemplating her murder even then? he wondered. Or was it something lurking below his consciousness? Something he had felt stirring, so that he had wanted Moore to stay with him—to keep it from happening?

He would never know, he realized, as the fires reached into his skull and consumed his brain.

As he awoke, feeling very weak upon white linen, the voice within his earphones was saying to Alvin Moore: ". . . Let that be a lesson to you."

Moore tore off the earphones with what he thought was a strong gesture, but his muscles responded weakly. Still, the earphones came off.

He opened his eyes and stared.

He might be in the Set's Sick Ward, located high up in the Hall of Sleep, or in hell. Franz Andrews, the attorney who had advised him to plead guilty, sat at his bedside.

"How do you feel?" he asked.

"Oh, great! Care to play a set of tennis?"

The man smiled faintly.

"You have successfully discharged your debt to society," he stated, "through the symbolic penalty procedure."

"Oh, that explains everything," said Moore wryly. Finally: "I don't see why there had to be any penalty, symbolic or otherwise. That rhymer murdered my wife."

"He'll pay for it," said Andrews.

Moore rolled onto his side and studied the dispassionate, flat-featured face at his elbow. The attorney's short hair was somewhere between blond and gray and his gaze unflinchingly sober.

"Do you mind repeating what you just said?"

"Not at all. I said he'd pay for it."

"He's not dead!"

"No, he's quite alive—two floors above us. His head has to heal before he can stand trial. He's too ill to face execution."

"He's alive!" said Moore. "Alive? Then what the hell was I executed for?"

"Well, you *did* kill the man," said Andrews, somewhat annoyed. "The fact that the doctors were later able to revive him does not alter the fact that a homicide occurred. The symbolic penalty exists for all such cases. You'll think twice before ever doing it again."

Moore tried to rise. He failed.

"Take it easy. You're going to need several more days of rest before you can get up. Your own revival was only last night."

Moore chuckled weakly. Then he laughed for a long, long time. He stopped, ending with a little sob.

"Feel better now?"

"Sure, sure," he whispered hoarsely. "Like a million bucks, or whatever the crazy currency is these days. What kind of execution will Unger get for murder?"

"Gas," said the attorney, "the same as you, if the alleged—"

"Symbolic, or for keeps?"

"Symbolic, of course."

Moore did not remember what happened next, except that he heard someone screaming and there was suddenly a medic whom he had not noticed doing something to his arm. He heard the soft hiss of an injection. Then he slept.

When he awakened he felt stronger and he noticed an insolent bar of sunlight streaking the wall opposite him. Andrews appeared not to have moved from his side.

He stared at the man and said nothing.

"I have been advised," said the attorney, "of your lack of knowledge concerning the present state of law in these matters. I did not stop to consider the length of your membership in the Set. These things so seldom occur—in fact, this is the first such case I've ever handled—that I simply assumed you knew what a symbolic penalty was when I spoke with you back in your cell. I apologize."

Moore nodded.

"Also," he continued, "I assumed that you had considered the circumstances under which Mister Unger allegedly committed a homicide—"

" 'Allegedly,' hell! I was there. He drove a stake through her heart!" Moore's voice broke at that point.

"It *was* to have been a precedent-making decision," said Andrews, "as to whether he was to be indicted now for attempted homicide, or be detained until after the operation and face homicide charges if things do not go well. The matter of his detention then would have raised many more problems—which were fortunately resolved at his own suggestion. After his recovery he will retire to his bunker and remain there until the nature of the offense had been properly determined. He has volunteered to do this of his own free will, so no legal decision was delivered on the matter. His trial is postponed, therefore, until some of the surgical techniques have been refined—"

"What surgical techniques?" asked Moore, raising himself into a seated position and leaning against the headboard.

His mind was fully alert for the first time since Christmas. He felt what was coming next.

He said one word.

"Explain."

Andrews shifted in his chair.

"Mister Unger," he began, "had a poet's conception as to the exact location of the human heart. He did not pierce it centrally, although the accidental angling of the stake did cause it to pass through the left ventricle. —That can be repaired easily enough, according to the medics.

"Unfortunately, however, the slanting of the shaft caused it to strike against her spinal column," he said, "smashing two vertebrae and cracking several others. It appears that the spinal cord was severed. . . ."

Moore was numb again, numb with the realization that had dawned as the lawyer's words were filling the air between them. Of course she wasn't dead. Neither was she alive. She was sleeping the cold sleep. The spark of life would remain within her until the arousal began. *Then*, and only then, could she die. Unless—

". . . Complicated by her pregnancy and the period of time necessary to raise her body temperature to an operable one," Andrews was saying.

"When are they going to operate?" Moore broke in.

"They can't say for certain, at this time," answered Andrews. "It will have to be a specially designed operation, as it raises problems for which there are answers in theory but not in practice. Any one of the factors could be treated at present, but the others couldn't be held in abeyance while the surgery is going on. Together, they are rather formidable—to repair the heart and fix the back, and to save the child, all at the same time, will require some new instrumentation and some new techniques."

"How long?" insisted Moore.

Andrews shrugged.

"They can't say. Months, years. She's all right as she is now, but—"

Moore asked him to go away, rather loudly, and he did.

* * *

The following day, feeling dizzy, he got to his feet and refused to return to bed until he could see Unger.

"He's in custody," said the medic who attended him.

"No he isn't," replied Moore. "You're not a lawyer, and I've already spoken with one. He won't be taken into legal custody until after he awakens from his next cold sleep—whenever that is."

It took over an hour for him to get permission to visit Unger. When he did, he was accompanied by Andrews and two orderlies.

"Don't you trust the symbolic penalty?" he smirked at Andrews. "You know that I'm supposed to think twice before I do it again."

Andrews looked away and did not answer him.

"Anyhow, I'm too weak and I don't have a hammer handy."

They knocked and entered.

Unger, his head turbaned in white, sat propped up by pillows. A closed book lay on the counterpane. He had been staring out of the window and into the garden. He turned his head toward them.

"Good morning, you son of a bitch," observed Moore.

"Please," said Unger.

Moore did not know what to say next. He had already expressed all that he felt. So he headed for the chair beside the bed and sat on it. He fished his pipe from the pocket of his robe and fumbled with it to hide his discomfort. Then he realized he had no tobacco with him. Neither Andrews nor the orderlies appeared to be watching them.

He placed the dry pipe between his teeth and looked up.

"I'm sorry," said Unger. "Can you believe that?"

"No," answered Moore.

"She's the future and she's yours," said Unger. "I drove a stake through her heart but she isn't really dead. They say they're working on the operating machines now. The doctors will fix up everything that I did, as good as new." He winced and looked down at the bedclothes.

"If it's any consolation to you," he continued, "I'm suffering and I'll suffer more. There is no Senta to save this Dutchman. I'm going to ride it out with the Set, or without

it, in a bunker—die in some foreign place among strangers.''
He looked up, regarding Moore with a weak smile. Moore
stared him back down. "They'll save her!" he insisted.
"She'll sleep until they're absolutely certain of the tech-
nique. Then you two will get off together and I'll keep on
going. You'll never see me after that. I wish you happiness.
I won't ask your forgiveness.''

Moore got to his feet.

"We've got nothing left to say. We'll talk again some year,
in a day or so.''

He left the room wondering what else he could have said.

"An ethical quesion has been put before the Set—that is
to say, myself,'' said Mary Maude. "Unfortunately, it was
posed by government attorneys, so it cannot be treated as
most ethical questions are to be treated. It requires an answer.''

"Involving Moore and Unger?" asked Andrews.

"Not directly. Involving the entire Set, as a result of their
escapade.''

She indicated the fac-sheet on her desk. Andrews nodded.

" 'Unto Us a Babe is Born,' '' she read, considering the
photo of the prostrate Setman in the church. "A front-page
editorial in this periodical has accused us of creating all va-
rieties of neurotics—from necrophilists on down the line.
Then there's that other photo—we still don't know who took
it—here, on page three—''

"I've seen it.''

"They now want assurances that ex-Setmen will remain
frivolous and not turn into eminent undesirables.''

"This is the first time it's ever happened—like this.''

"Of course,'' she smiled. "they're usually decent enough
to wait a few weeks before going anti-social—and wealth
generally compensates for most normal maladjustments. But,
according to the accusations, we are either selecting the wrong
people—which is ridiculous—or not mustering them out
properly when they leave—which is profoundly ridiculous.
First, because I do all the interviewing, and second, because
you *can't* boot a person half a century or so into the future
and expect him to land on his feet as his normal, cheerful

self, regardless of any orientation you may give him. Our people make a good show of it, though, because they don't generally do much of anything.

"But both Moore and Unger were reasonably normal, and they never knew each other particularly well. Both watched a little more closely than most Setmen as their worlds became history, and both were highly sensitive to those changes. Their problem, though, was interpersonal."

Andrews said nothing.

"By that, I mean it was a simple case of jealousy over a woman—an unpredictable human variable. I could not have foreseen their conflict. The changing times have nothing to do with it. Do they?"

Andrews did not answer.

". . . Therefore, there is no problem," she continued. "We are not dumping Kaspar Hausers onto the street. We are simply transplanting wealthy people of good taste a few generations into the future—and they get on well. Our only misstep so far was predicated upon a male antagonism of the mutually accelerating variety, caused by a beautiful woman. That's all. Do you agree?"

"He thought that he was really going to die . . ." said Andrews. "I didn't stop to think that he knew nothing of the World Legal Code."

"A minor matter," she dismissed it. "He's still living."

"You should have seen his face when he came to in the Clinic."

"I'm not interested in faces. I've seen too many. Our problem now is to manufacture a problem and then to solve it to the government's satisfaction."

"The world changes so rapidly that I almost need to make a daily adjustment to it myself. These poor—"

"Some things do not change," said Mary Maude, "but I can see what you're driving at. Very clever. We'll hire us an independent Psych Team to do us a study indicating that what the Set needs is more adjustment, and they'll recommend that one day be set aside every year for therapeutic purposes. We'll hold each one in a different part of the world—at a non-Party locale. Lots of cities have been screaming for concessions. They'll all be days spent doing simple, adjustive things, mingling with un-Set people. Then, in the evening we'll have a light meal, followed by casual, restful entertainment, and then some dancing—dancing's good for the psyche, it relaxes tensions. —I'm sure that will satisfy all parties concerned." She smiled at the last.

"I believe you are right," said Andrews.

"Of course. After the Psych Team writes several thousand pages, you'll draft a few hundred of your own to summarize the findings and cast them into the form of a resolution to be put before the board."

He nodded.

"I thank you for your suggestions."

"Any time. That's what I'm paid for."

After he had left, Mary Maude donned her black glove and placed another log on the fire. Genuine logs cost more and more every year, but she did not trust flameless heaters.

It was three days before Moore had recovered sufficiently to enter the sleep again. As the prep-injection dulled his senses and his eyes closed, he wondered what alien judgment day would confront him when he awakened. He knew, though, that whatever else the new year brought, his credit would be good.

He slept, and the world passed by.

Elegy For Angels and Dogs

WALTER JON WILLIAMS

The lights went out and the party (or the Party) started (or recommenced). Cao Cao gave Lamoral a cigar.

"It's a boy," he said in his slight, charming, Oxonian lisp. The band began to play a slow dance, the light gravity permitting little else.

Lamoral stuck the cigar in his polymerized cuirass. In the computer-enhanced view granted by his high-tech spectacles, Cao Cao's skin was a brilliant orange and his teeth were green. His name, at least to a Westerner, was pronounced as that of a black-tongued Chinese dog.

"The child isn't even born yet," Lamoral said.

"These days, 1A, that's strictly a formality."

"My dance," said Carolly, and Lamoral swept her away, leaving orange Cao Cao in his wake.

Back on Earth, and indeed everywhere, it was Shakespeare's birthday.

X marked the spot, the spot being Ariel, the X a grand feature upon it. The light of the sun, such as it was, was insignificant this far out. Seen without video specs Uranus was a creamy, featureless blue, Ariel was umber, the rings were black, and Titania, Miranda, and Umbriel, suspended in one corner of the sky or another, were black-upon-black. With the shades, it was as if Oberon—the King of Faërie was currently eclipsed by Uranus—had waved his majestic hand and created a polychrome miracle. Giant Uranus dazzled across half the sky, green and red, with little silver clouds floating on its surface. The rings, a series of wedding bands mating the old castrated Creator to his consorts, were a brilliant gold. Frost blazed silver on the piled-up ramparts of the X. The satellites overhead seemed to churn with color.

"Cao Cao's such a bastard," said Carolly. "You're stepping on my feet."

"Sorry. I was watching the sky."

"You used to have eyes only for me."

Lamoral looked at her. "That was before your skin turned its current carrot shade."

"Turn off your glasses."

Lamoral did so. The Party Set, dressed as characters from Shakespeare's comedies, danced dimly in the dark. Scene, Lamoral thought, from *The Bard in Hell*.

"You're still stepping on me."

"Beg pardon. Now I can't see anything at all."

"You're off your stride, Lamoral." She sighed. "And so am I. Let's get something to drink."

There was an insistent draft on his knees. He was Theseus; she was a hopeful Rosalind in green hose, though a bit old for the part. His Attic Majesty's armor rattled as he handed her bright hippocras. They moved toward the rim of the Party Barge. Miranda swirled past, crowned by wildflowers, pursued by a lustful Aguecheek. Carolly crooked an eyebrow.

"A lot of Mirandas out tonight." Tartly.

"What's he got, d'you suppose?"

"Cao Cao?"

A brittle laugh keened above the music: one of the Mirandas. The sound seemed a little too frantic for this early in the evening.

"Lilt," said Carolly, answering his question. Her voice dripped acid.

Lamoral's twin brother Alexander, playing at being the

Duke of Vienna playing at being a friar, rotated past with Indira Batish, who was one of the constellation of Mirandas. Later in the evening Alex would reveal his true ducal majesty; there was lace winking like silver from under his habit.

"Your brother dances better than you." Carolly's voice was still pungent.

"He's not as distracted."

"At least you didn't blame your partner. I thank you for that."

At the edge of the transparent dome of the Party Barge was a silhouette. A brocade Tudor coif framed a waterfall of dark hair.

"Sandy," said Lamoral.

Her gown rustled as she turned. Her dark face was pale against the black-dusted walls of Ariel's X. Long-fingered hands were folded gracefully over her belly.

"A lovely costume," Carolly said.

"Thank you," said Sandrea Salazar.

"The source isn't immediately apparent."

"Queen Hermione."

There was a hopeful pause as each tried to remember the appropriate play.

"Excuse me." Sandrea bobbed a half-curtsey and swept away into the swaying Set.

Lamoral looked after her. "I wonder," he said, the track of a thought that never really lighted.

"Winter's Tale," said a new voice. Wayne Unger appeared, dressed as Robin Goodfellow. His high-tech specs somehow enhanced, rather than spoiled, the illusion.

Lamoral tried to remember if he'd ever read the play in question.

"Queen Hermione," Unger prompted. "Poor lady. A wronged woman altogether."

Which, Lamoral decided, summed it up.

The Party Set was back, better than ever! That was the message being sent from the Party Barge, the tour of Uranus's moons. Forget the Crash of '30! The Bad Decade was over, and taste and elegance once again reigned supreme.

"Does it make you want to climb again, Lamoral?" Puck,

fiddling with the settings on his shades, peered out of what Lamoral had christened the Party Barge. Behind him, Carolly gazed fitfully at the unchanging landscape.

"Mount those extraterrestrial cliffs?" Unger went on. "Plant your footprints atop those airless peaks?" An ocean had passed his lips this night; he was swaying as if with the tide.

"Not really."

"Not to the conquerer of K2, of Olympus Mons? The sight of those walls don't make you swoon with desire to reassemble a new version of the old triumvirate?"

"Hormayr's dead."

"I know, but—"

"He's still dead."

Unger gave a heavy sight. "I'm disappointed."

"Climbing in light gravity is dead easy. I could probably bound up the sides of the X in a couple jumps. I might even end up in orbit."

Unger smiled. "Climbers should always use a safety line." Lamoral contemplated his drink and thought of Hormayr. "So we should."

"I was hoping you'd want to make the attempt, so I could talk you into taking me with you. I'd like to replace Hormayr, at least for this one climb."

Lamoral looked at him for a moment and wondered whether or not to take this seriously. Unger, somewhat to Lamoral's surprise, seemed perfectly sincere.

"Why Ariel?" he said finally.

"I think it's the black snow. The idea is so . . . passionless, if you know what I mean. All the effort, just to plant your feet on ashes. The burnt-out ends of smoky days . . . And, up there, dead silence. Just hydrogen crying in your headphones."

"Thoughts of a dry brain in a dry season," said Carolly. Dryly.

Unger looked sulky.

"Just write the poem, Unger," Carolly advised.

"Sometimes one needs the experience."

"You could ask Alex," Lamoral said. "He's as good a climber as I am."

"Your twin is too cheerful. He would intrude." Unger seemed hurt by Lamoral's refusal.

"Sorry," said Lamoral, not sorry at all. He possessed no desire whatever to venture into that soul-sapping twilight.

Unger reached into his jerkin and pulled out one of Cao Cao's cigars. He lit it and stared out the ship's dome.

"My glass is empty," said Carolly.

"Let's refill it."

The poet remained behind fiddling with his spectacles, turning dark into light and back again.

His job, after all.

Set dances had grown longer and more intricate, on the theory they should be the sort of thing only Set members could do. The theory was fallacious, since the rest of the world had a lot more time to practice, not having months to sleep between engagements. The dancers' patterns were not therefore without flaw, but at least the mistakes were made with style, and it was difficult to tell an honest error from an inspired improvisation. The dances had been adapted for low gravity: couples formed little solar systems, orbited each other at arm's length, their opposing velocities keeping them anchored in space, preventing an excess of enthusiasm from shooting them like cannonballs into the dome of the Party Barge.

"Been talking to our only convicted murderer?"

Thomas Edwardes and his partner were at the end of the set major, waiting to reenter the dance at the beginning of the next figure. Edwardes was dressed as some noble Elizabethan personage or other, a cap with a feather tilted over one ear, a sword at his side.

"You speak," said Lamoral, "as if there are others who haven't been convicted."

Edwardes winked.

"It strikes me," said Carolly, "that murder is far too intimate an act for our subject to participate in directly. I'm sure he hired it done."

Edwardes gave a brittle, all-too-familiar laugh: Lilt. The awaited figure came, and he stepped into the dance. Carolly and Lamoral refilled their glasses and watched the Party Set move in their orbits.

The dance came to an end. Alex and Indira Batish came giggling toward the bar. "I was telling Alex," Indira said to Lamoral, "that the two of you should have come as the Ephesian and Syracusan Antipholuses. Or is it Antipholi?"

"Antipholoi, I think," said Lamoral.

"Whichever. You should have done it."

"We get mistaken for each other enough as it is."

"Not by me."

Alex smirked. "Are you sure, my dear? It was dark, that Midwinter's Eve. Or so Lamoral told me."

Indira raised an eyebrow. "I've told you apart in the dark before. Why shouldn't I have then?"

Alex clutched his chest and mock-staggered. Indira smiled and asked for wine.

The orchestra began again. Lamoral espied, in the darkness, the wronged Queen of Sicilia.

He made his excuses and followed.

"Join the dance?"

"I don't think so, 1A. I'm not in the mood."

At her voice Lamoral's heart gave an indecent little lurch. He told it to behave itself.

"Cao Cao insists on calling me that," he said. "May I hope you won't follow his example?"

"But—to quote someone or other in the dim, dear past— you can look it up."

"Only if you browse through the *Almanach de Gotha*. Not your sort of reading, I'd think."

She gave him a look. "But it's *your* sort, isn't it? And so it must be with the other 1As. Just because they're 1As. They can't help it, and neither can you."

"I'm not here," said Lamoral, "to talk about me."

"You never are."

"Are you sure you won't dance?"

Sandrea Salazar sized him up for a long moment, then held out her arms, the hands dangling, puppetlike. "Do your worst," she said.

He swung her onto the floor in a series of cool, precise orbits. "You don't have to leave the Set," he said.

"I'm leaving because I want to."

"It's not—" He searched for words. How to tell her that he knew her for a creature of impulse, that this impulse to leave the Party Set and bear her child was one she would regret? She was not in the mood for dancing, which meant she was already beginning to regret; but of course she wouldn't admit it. She was going to be stubborn until it was too late.

"The Set was made for you, Sandy," he said. "You delight us all with your presence. Speaking purely out of my own self-interest—"

"As you always do . . ."

"I'll miss you."

Her long eyes looked up into his from beneath soaring wings of elaborate stage makeup. "Try to bear up," she said.

Lamoral surrendered. "I will say no more whilst this fey spirit is upon you."

They orbited for a while in silence. Lamoral thought about Sandy, Cao Cao, and murder. He would have to do better than Unger: it would have to be something better than a stake through the heart this time.

Silly to kill a person over someone he didn't love.

And he didn't love her, right?

"I haven't been gone from the real world for too long," Sandrea said. "I can fit in again."

"As well as you ever did," he said. Knowing she never had.

Sandrea seemed to understand his meaning. "It'll be different. I'll have a child," she said.

"A boy, or so I hear."

"The child will anchor me in time. Give me a sense of things."

"Things. The *usual* things, Sandy. That's the alternative to the Set."

"I'm tired of hearing this."

"Do you know 'Portrait d'une Femme?' '. . . the usual thing: one dull man, dulling and uxorious, one average mind—with one thought less, each year.' You may be condemning yourself to that.''

"I won't have just one man, dull or otherwise. And I don't think I want to dance any more.'' She turned and made her way off the floor; Lamoral followed in his clanking armor.

Two Party Set months ago—two decades realtime?—Sandy had walked out on a rich second husband who'd adored her, been showered with money in the settlement—he wanted her back and was still full of irrational hope—and then gone into the Party Set with Carolly as sponsor while her poor ex floundered hopelessly at the portals, turned down by the Doyenne despite his loot.

Now Sandrea was walking out again.

Maybe, Lamoral thought, he was being persistent only because he couldn't believe this was happening to *him*. Maybe that second husband had been just as surprised.

Sandy spun toward him; her eyes were bright.

"It's the Set that has one thought less each year," she said. "Less and less connection with reality! Fewer real connections even with each other! I want to feel something real for a change!"

"This is real," Lamoral said. "This is really Ariel, that's really Uranus up there. If you step outside the Party Barge without a suit, you'll die."

She looked at him. "The boy's not yours."

"I know."

"You don't have any responsibility here."

"I want you to stay."

"Because you're selfish. We've established that."

"You don't have to have the child. We should establish that as well."

"I won't abort."

"There are alternatives. The boy can be brought to term in an automatic womb, given to foster parents."

"I want something that's *mine*!'' Tears were wrecking her elaborate makeup job. "There's nothing here that's *mine*!'' Lamoral regretted the lack of a handkerchief in his armor.

It was Carolly who came to the rescue, producing a scrap of lace from inside her Robin Hood hat. "Careful, children,'' she said. "There are eyes everywhere.''

Sandrea blew lustily. "It's my party," she said. "I'll cry if I want to."

Carolly looked suspiciously at Lamoral and then Sandrea, trying to decide who was to blame for all this latest sadness. In the end she took Sandrea's arm and took her off for consolation. Lamoral gave a false, chivalrous smile and bowed farewell. He considered the consolations of homicide.

A Lilt-laughing Miranda approached, and Lamoral spun her out onto the floor. After the orchestra faded away, Lamoral was approached by his brother. "Edwardes keeps looking at me and rattling his rapier," Alex said. "I think he's sung *Otello* too damn often. Desdemona's left the Set, so he's got no one left to murder but me."

"You should be accustomed to jealous swains by now."

"Good grief. It was *years* ago. I'm with Indira now."

"It was only a few weeks ago, our time."

"I wish he'd grow up." Petulantly. "He challenged me to a duel, did I tell you that?"

"I believe you mentioned something of the sort." To anyone who'd listen, in fact.

"On some asteroid or other where it wasn't illegal. Just the two of us, our pistols, and maybe a hundred ships in orbit, all full of gawkers and video cameras."

"I doubt he was serious, Alex. Probably just Lilt talking."

"He's singing tonight." Alex tried to look smug. "I'm going to enjoy hearing the famous voice as it begins to show its age."

Cao Cao appeared, Prospero with a box of cigars. "It's a boy," he said.

Alex took a blue-banded stogie.

"I've got one, thanks," said Lamoral.

"Please have another, 1A."

"I don't smoke much." Wondering if the lisp was affected or whether Cao Cao had actually allowed himself a small imperfection.

"Got to keep those lungs in shape, I suppose." Cao Cao smiled with perfect teeth. "Never know when you're going to take another shot at Changabang."

Lamoral gave earnest mental consideration to how Cao Cao would look bouncing down Changabang's crumbling west wall. But Cao Cao kept turning into Karl-August Hormayr, and Lamoral forced the image from his mind.

Smiling Cao Cao was the son of a Shanghai police sergeant who had retired from the force a multi-millionaire. He had been raised in a picturesque tax haven at Lagrange Point Four, insulated from his father's former associates by a squad of elegantly-dressed and unusually lethal bodyguards. Cao Cao trained in biochemistry and, according to his official biography, invented Lilt, the world's most perfect intoxicant, before his thirtieth birthday. The unofficial grapevine suggested instead that Cao Cao had appropriated the formula from some hapless inventor, who had then perished in some quiet and convenient fashion at the hands of fastidious Chinese hitmen dressed in monochrome tie-and-tails and white doeskin gloves. The old Shanghai connection had proved useful in marketing the stuff, although eventually Lilt, which had fewer drawbacks than any other known consciousness-altering substance, was legalized throughout most of human-inhabited space; and Cao Cao, his business legitimized, sat back to happily collect his royalties and to join the Party Set.

Lamoral gave Cao Cao a smile. "Have you made plans for the boy?"

"Of course." Cao Cao stuck one of his own cigars in his too-handsome face. "Trust fund, the works. And a guardian, when Sandy gets tired of having a child around and finds another whim to pursue."

Lamoral absorbed this coldly. With calculation, he broadened his smile. "Planning on sending him into the family business, then?"

Cao Cao's hand, holding a gold lighter, froze for just an instant on its path to the cigar. Cao Cao puffed the cigar into life, then looked up at Lamoral.

"At least my family *has* a business."

And stalked away.

Alex smirked. "Game point, I'd say."

Lamoral watched the retreating Prospero with mixed annoyance and satisfaction. Pity the man hadn't stuck around for set and match: Lamoral had a strong volley and a wicked verbal backhand.

"His facts weren't even correct," he said, principally for

the benefit of whatever state-of-the-art eavesdroppers might be lurking beneath the dome. "Our family has *lots* of businesses."

"I hope it was more than a bad stock tip that sent Cao Cao storming off," Kitsune Takami said as she ambled out of the crowd around the bar. She was perhaps the tallest person in the room, having been, among other things, a basketball star. Knowing she would look absurd in a farthingale, she had adopted Elizabethan drag, a fashion kinder to her lanky form. Long blueblack hair poured over a short ruff; a lacy gold pomander hung around her neck on a chain. She wore a ducal crown upon which rioted strawberry leaves made of delicately-fashioned gold.

Alex swept her a bow and kissed her knuckles. "It was a thing of beauty, milady. Lamoral skewered him where it hurts, right in his ancestors."

"Congratulations."

"I'm looking forward to the next engagement."

Kitsune raised the pomander to her nose, took a delicate period sniff. Her eyes followed Cao Cao. "I was afraid it would take murder to get to him, though I confess I couldn't decide who the exact victim should be, Cao Cao or Sandy. But Sandy is doing herself in, or nearly, by leaving the Set, and that simplifies the decision."

"What's your chosen weapon?" Alex seemed delighted by this news. "Knife? Poison?" He leaned closer to her. "A stake through the heart?"

Kitsune smiled. "Words, I think. On reflection I've decided that the best revenge is simply telling the world what I learned about Cao Cao during and subsequent to our . . ." She smiled and took another sniff. "Our little *folie*."

Alex gave a conspiratorial smile. "Though Cao Cao and I have barely been aware of one another on a personal level, I confess to having developed an aesthetic objection to his manner of operation. The way he dumped you was simply appalling."

Kitsune looked at him. "An interesting comment, coming from one of the Set's most expert heartbreakers."

"An expert is entitled to criticize the loutish amateurs that cross his path. Were you and I, milady," kissing her hand once more, "to become involved, and were I to see the necessity of ending our relationship, I'd do it with much more grace. You'd have no reason to plot murder. We would probably, in fact, remain good friends."

Kitsune gazed down at Alex with a certain amount of calculation in her eyes.

"No offense, Alex," Lamoral said, "but I'd like to interrupt your hypothetical affaire, if you don't mind, and get straight to the dirt. Cao Cao is probably going to try to counterattack sooner or later, and I'd like to have my salvo ready."

Kitsune retrieved her hand. "Liu Shuyuan," she said.

Lamoral looked at her. "Is that all?"

"Just mention the name. That should do the job nicely."

"Drop the name in Cao Cao's path," Alex said with glee, "and watch him turn pale. If there are any eavesdroppers, they'll be overwhelmed with curiosity."

"There may be eavesdroppers now," said Lamoral.

"If there are," simply, "then they're curious."

"There probably aren't, you know," Kitsune said. "We're so many light-hours from Earth that there's no way the listeners could ever control their devices. They'd have to plant them all over the place, and the crew has had four months to sweep the Barge clean."

"True," Lamoral said. "I hadn't realized." He considered Cao Cao once more. "Any more arrows in your quiver?"

"That one arrow should suffice for the man who once sent Mary Maude Mullen a dog skewered on a spit." Kitsune gave a secret smile. "I'll save the rest for a time when we're absolutely certain no one's listening. I'm quite beside myself anticipating Cao Cao's reaction when he begins to think everyone in the Set knows his secrets."

"He'll know where these bulletins are coming from."

"Some of them, yes, the few he told me about. Others are available to anyone willing to do the research."

"And Liu Shuyuan?"

"Not pillowtalk, my dear. I've had almost three years real-time for my detectives to do their work. Cao Cao has enemies outside the Set, and a lot of them were talkative."

Lamoral was impressed by the thoroughness of Kitsune's

work. "I'm surprised they're not all dead. A lot of years have passed on the outside."

"It's precisely because some of them are dead that others can talk." She took another whiff off her pomander. "The triads are fueled by their own mythology, and myths are by their nature transmitted orally. Gangsters can talk about anyone who's dead, or anyone who's become a legend; and Cao Cao, being a member of the Set, shares qualities with both."

Lamoral considered this. "Did you encounter actual evidence of crime? Could Cao Cao end up in jail on account of this?"

Kitsune shook her head. "All myth amounts to is organized hearsay. Nothing verifiable." She gave a smile as cold as the ammonia frost outside. "There's just enough to make him acutely uncomfortable so long as he remains in the public eye."

"Drive him out of the Set?" Alex smiled. "Magnificent, milady. My congratulations. If I ever find myself forced to break your heart, I will make certain to do it with particular delicacy."

Lamoral left Alex and Kitsune outlining the finish to their as-yet-unrealized relationship and paced back to the bar. Cao Cao compelled to leave the Set? Lamoral was uncertain whether or not that was desirable. It left Cao Cao out in the real world with Sandy.

Years would pass outside, though, before Kitsune's whispering campaign bore fruit, assuming it ever did. Sandy might be ten years older, and Cao Cao would have other things to think about—whether any of his old enemies were still alive, for one thing.

At the bar Lamoral filled his glass with a Trockenbeeren Auslese from his own family vinyards at Rauenthal. Living in the Party Set, a few nights each year, he could still keep track of his vintages. Crisp, he thought as he sipped, rather mellow for a Rhenish. They were going to be paying high prices for this stuff back home. Savoring the wine, he headed for the edge of the dome.

There stood Sandy, her elaborate headdress silhouetted blackly against the pale blue of Uranus. Unger was before her on his knees, clutching her hand. There were tears running out from beneath his video specs. "Will the veiled sister . . ." he began, and his voice drowned in sobs. He began again. "Will the veiled sister between the slender/ Yew trees pray for those who offend her/ And are terrified and cannot surrender . . ."

"Up, Unger." Lamoral wanted to kick him.

"Will the sister." Sobbing again. "Kissed her. Mist her." Lamoral looked at Sandy. "Let's get out of here."

"It's all right." There was a surprising gentleness in her voice. "He's just drunk."

"He's always drunk."

"But I'm an *honest* drunk," said Unger. He was trying to rise and not succeeding. "An honest drunk *on* an honest drunk. An honest drunk being one you *pay for.* Not like—" One foot gave way and he sprawled Arielward. "Not like what the Mephisto of the triads peddles. Not like that Lilt. With no hangover. No liver-rot. No honest purging." He clutched at the floor; the smooth surface gave him no purchase. "No real feelings at all," he said. "Nothing to keep you sane. Just joy, and then nothing. A fantasy drunk, all air."

"Pass out, Unger," said Lamoral, "and get it over with."

Sandy looked at Lamoral in annoyance. "Help me get him to a chair."

"There is no awe in Lilt," Unger said as Lamoral picked him up like a doll—the light gravity helped—and tried to set him upright. "No grandiosity. No pity or terror. I know I'm pathetic." Unger was weeping again, having changed tack. He fell in slow motion toward the floor. Lamoral, giving up, let him go. Unger landed on his back and belched. Lamoral became acutely aware of the high level of Unger's garlic consumption. "But pathetic is something real," he said. "It may not be heroic, or tragic, but it's real. Without tragedy, you can have no dimension, and without dimension, no humanity. And there are no tragedies on Lilt." He blinked up at them. "Am I getting through?"

Lamoral looked at Sandy. "It's hopeless," he said. "He wants to be here; let him stay."

"I'll stay with him," Sandy said.

If Lamoral remained another minute he'd strangle some-

one, though he wasn't certain just who. He headed for the
dance floor again, drained his glass, put the glass on the bar.
He turned on his video shades, hoping it would brighten his
mood. He intended to dance for the next ten hours, then sleep
for at least six months.

The orchestra faded out to scattered applause, and people
cleared the floor. The orchestra struck up something that was
definitely not the prelude to a dance tune. A spotlight picked
out Thomas Edwardes. His doublet was unbuttoned and his
massive black torso gleamed in the light.

"*Otello* again," said someone. "God, he's in a rut."

"He's singing with a new Lilt these days," said another
wag.

Not true. The voice was magnificent, the acting superb.
Alex was bound to be disappointed: there wasn't a thing
wrong with the voice, no hesitation, no flat notes on the highs,
no unexpected diminuendi.

Sweat popped from Otello's broad forehead. He'd just made
up his mind to slaughter his bride. His hands clutched con-
vincingly at an invisible throat. Lamoral wondered whose
throat the old boy had in mind.

Ora e per sempre addio . . .

Now and forever, Lamoral translated, farewell to peace of
mind.

Lamoral hoped to hell this was not an omen.

Lamoral could only trust that the cameras were turned off
by the time Robin Goodfellow upchucked into the punch
bowl. Well before that the ball had begun to degenerate: Set
members jumped to and fro in the low gravity, caroming off
the dome and scattering party favors on the mortals below.
Though this particular fiesta was supposed to go on for another few "moons"—there would be a different installment
of the Party at each of Uranus' satellites—Lamoral decided
that he was not having a good time, and that he'd head for
the cold bunkers and leave instructions to wake him in time
for the Day of the Dead celebration in Guadalajara next November.

Once out from under the dome, he walked through corridors straight off a 19th-century P&O steamer, all P.O.S.H.

The interior corridors were panelled in teak, the carpets were from India, the fixtures were brass, and the cabins featured nautical art on the walls and little brass nameplates on the doors—on Lamoral's was not only his name but his armorial bearings, with the angel, the towers and the spitted dog that had so amused Kitsune. The Party Barge was actually the *Queen Mary*, a name that referred to Mary Maude Mullen rather than to any member of the House of Windsor. The Barge's name was one which Lamoral, for various reasons having to do with pedigree, declined to employ.

Lamoral's cabin was bigger than that of any steamer ever built. Lamoral took off his armor and his video glasses and dropped them on the carpet for the robots to pick up. Cao Cao's forgotten cigar tumbled from the cuirass and rolled on the floor. After he put on the white jumpsuit most Setmen wore into their bunkers, Lamoral drank another glass of the Rauenthal, then picked up the cigar, lit it, and headed for the bunkers.

In the corridor he made a turn and saw Indira Batish just ahead, walking in the same direction. He caught up with her and said hello. She gave him a look; he saw her caste mark was back in place. "When do you next wake?" she asked.

"El Día de los Muertos."

"I'm waiting for Buddha to descend from the Tishita Heaven on a flight of stairs."

"Where's he doing that?"

"Lhasa. November, I think."

"I may see you there. I've never seen the Buddha walk down from Heaven before."

"I'm not sure he does it publicly."

The sound of voices resonated down the corridor, from the lounge where other Setfolk were waiting for their prep shots to take effect. Lamoral recognized Unger's belching rumble, Edwardes' trained, resonant voice. Indira and Lamoral walked past the lounge to the pre-sleep clinic and looked inside for Jameson, the medic. He wasn't to be seen, though the injector was lying on a table with a box of ampoules beside it. One door, open, led to the lounge; another, closed, to the cold bunkers. Lamoral and Indira returned to the lounge.

"Jameson?" Lamoral saw the medic bent over Wayne Unger, who was lying in apparent comfort on the carpeted floor of the lounge, his video shades still shrouding his eyes. Sitting on the furniture in various postures of languor were Carolly and Kitsune, in identical white jumpsuits, and Edwardes, still in Elizabethan togs with a very modern fluffy towel around his neck.

"In a minute." Jameson offered Lamoral a thin smile. "I've got to talk Mr. Unger into investing in a new liver."

"Convince me it's an honest move," said Unger. "Convince me I'm not cheating my well-deserved fate."

"No one," said Kitsune Takami, obviously bored by this act, "joins the Set to die. If you wanted to shuffle off, you could have done it much more easily just by living on in your own time."

"Just by joining the Set, Unger, you cheat the Reaper," said Edwardes. "You might as well keep on cheating." Lilt kept dragging the corners of his mouth into a smile, though the rest of him was clearly not happy.

"Now that I think about it," Kitsune said, "you've cheated death at least three times. Once when you joined the Set, once when you beat that murder rap, once when Moore beat your brains out. No reason not to try for a fourth."

There was a moment of uncomfortable silence.

"Who was it," Carolly wondered, "who said that God looks after drunks, madmen, and the United States of America?"

Finally Unger gave a baffled nod. "A Daniel come to judgment! O wise young judge Kitsune how I do honor thee!" He waved his arms. "Bring on the new liver. The others may watch the operation if they desire. Perhaps they will be able to discern the future from inspection of my vitals."

"*Your* future," Carolly said, "almost certainly."

Jameson rose from his crouch. "I hope you're going to remember this resolution when you sober up, Mr. Unger." He looked up at Lamoral. "I can't give you your prep, Alex, till you've finished the cigar." He winked at Indira. "The lady I can shoot full of juice any time."

Lamoral had forgotten he wasn't supposed to smoke after taking the prep shot: he didn't smoke often enough for the rule to have made much of an impression on him. He didn't bother to correct Jameson's case of mistaken identity; he merely nodded and returned to the corridor. Indira went with Jameson to get her shot. Lamoral could hear voices fading in and out, moving between the clinic and the lounge.

Lamoral had smoked his cigar halfway when Alex turned a corner and headed toward him. Alex was dressed in the same type of anonymous white jumpsuit Lamoral wore, and was likewise smoking one of Cao Cao's cigars; Alex gave a half-wave as he walked past, then walked in through the clinic door. A few moments later he came out.

"Forgot I couldn't smoke," he said.

"Me, too."

"This party's already boring."

"I agree."

Alex chose a likely spot of wall and lounged against it. Lamoral tapped ash into his hand, Alex into the carpet. Conversation from the lounge faded in and out. None of it seemed very interesting.

Lamoral's cigar was almost finished when Cao Cao arrived. The chemist's jumpsuit was a custom number, red silk, with silver Chinese characters. Lamoral thought about Liu Shuyuan and gave an inward smile. Pity the exchange wouldn't be recorded.

But Cao Cao just walked past with a nod and a half-smile, then went into the lounge. Lamoral felt a trickle of disappointment.

Oh, well. Next time would be better; there would be recordings.

Alex puffed smoke into the corridor. His voice came out of a gunmetal cloud.

"I think I'll visit Regensburg when we get back."

"It's been a while since you've seen Gloria."

"I'd prefer not to. The depression after such a visit is a pall that lasts far, far too long."

"Family," Lamoral said, and gave him a meaningful look.

Alex offered a reluctant nod. "Family," he said. "Very well."

The voices from the lounge dwindled as people made their way to the cold bunkers. Lamoral finished his cigar and

walked to the clinic for his shot. "Hi, Alex," Jameson said.
"You must be drunker than you look, not remembering about
the cigar even after I told you the first time."

Lamoral dumped his cigar ash into the waste and rolled
up his sleeve. "I'm not Alex," he said.

Jameson smirked. "Pull the other one," he said.

Jameson put the hypogun to Lamoral's arm, fired it, and
made a note in the computer file to that effect. Rolling down
his sleeve, Lamoral went back out into the corridor to finish
passing the time with Alex. He didn't feel like being shut up
in the lounge with Cao Cao.

Alex finished his cigar and went into the clinic for his shot.
Time passed. The mild sedative added to the prep shot began
to drift slowly through Lamoral's mind. Tension began to ebb
away. He and Alex passed their time in silence.

He made his way to the cold bunker, closed his eyes, let
the machine do its work.

He would rise from his coffin on the Day of the Dead.

Legions of skeletons danced through his icicle dreams.

There was a different, yet familiar taste to walking. Someone had added Lilt to the formula. His brain, somewhat dis-
connected from his consciousness, rollicked in ecstasy as
warming blood was pumped through his body.

Eventually the pleasure settled down to an energizing background hum. Lungs brought in warm, effervescent air, air
that tasted faintly of champagne. Lamoral let the lid hiss back
and blinked in reality.

He could tell from the decor that his cold bunker had been
moved from the Party Barge back to Bermuda. There was a
young woman, in a Party Set jumpsuit, watching him from a
chair. He rose.

"Sorry if I bored you," he said. "I must have dozed off
for a moment."

She gave a deferent smile. "A little more than a moment,
your royal highness," she said, "but that's all right."

"I'm not a Royal," he said, for maybe the thousandth
time. "I'm a Serene."

"Oh. Sorry." She seemed flustered. She was pale-skinned

and dark-haired, attractive in her own way, but clearly not a candidate for the Set.

"Happens all the time," he assured her. He legged out of the bunker and stood up. He went to the clothing locker and opened it. A red-spotted skull mask looked out at him.

His costume for the Day of the Dead. Well.

"Your serene highness . . ." Uncertainly.

"Call me Lamoral." Smiling over his shoulder. "Everyone does."

"My name is Planter," the young woman said. "I'm here to assist with your new Adjustment."

"So soon? I was Adjusted back in January." He pushed the costume aside and looked for appropriate casual wear.

"You've been asleep a little longer than planned," Planter said.

Lamoral's hand froze on a seersucker suit. "The date?" he said.

"October thirty-first."

On time at least, Lamoral thought, for the Day of the Dead.

"Twenty-one forty-four," Planter finished.

Six years, Lamoral thought. Six years since the Party Set visited Ariel. He spun to face his Adjuster. "Why?" he asked.

"There's been a war. The Party Set decided . . ."

"Where?"

"Beg pardon?"

"Where was the war!" Lamoral clenched his fists.

"Oh. Everywhere. Earth, Luna, the satellites . . ."

"Europe?"

"Not really. Europe was sort of ignored after the Spanish launching facility was occupied by neutral troops." Planter seemed startled by his vehemence. "If you'll just sit down, I can . . ."

"South America?"

"Yes. It was particularly bad there. If you'll . . ."

"North America?"

"Yes. Well, parts." She seemed to have recovered herself; a smoothness had entered her voice. "If you'll sit down, I can bring you up to date and we can talk about . . ."

"I'll need a comm link," Lamoral said. "I'll also need a

monitor giving quotes from the London, Tokyo, and New York exchanges.''

"You don't have to worry about your investments, sir," Planter said. "The Party Set's Investment Intelligence managed our portfolio very well throughout the conflict."

"I have most of my investments outside the Set."

"Oh." She blinked. "No one told me."

"Just get me to a comm link. And get my brother."

Planter rose from her chair. "Yes. I suppose I can . . . I mean—"

"Just do it."

She resigned herself to her patient remaining maladjusted. "Yes, sir."

Lamoral's younger sister seemed to have aged two decades in the eight or so objective years since he'd seen her. That was always hard to take, seeing her youth vanish in installments, like a subject of time-lapse photography. She was in her sixties now, and had the benefit of the latest life-preservation technology, but still time had clawed her. The horrors of the war she described seemed abstract compared with the ravages made on her face and body, distanced though they were by the oval gold frame of the video screen, one that did double duty as a mirror when it wasn't showing the slightly-unreal outside to the slightly-unreal members of the Set.

"In the old days," Gloria said, "we would have finished off the war in a year or two. But no one had fought a war in over a century, and we went about it all wrong. All three sides blundered throughout, and finally two blundered into mutual disaster and the third declared victory before the others had the strength to dispute it."

"Who fought?" Lamoral said. "Who won?"

There was a touch of severity in Gloria's flinty eyes. "No one you know, dear."

Alex vented a humorless chuckle. Gloria's eyes flickered across the video screen to him, then back to Lamoral. Behind her were the functional confines of her office in the Schloss St. Emmeram.

"What did it cost?" Lamoral asked.

"Two hundred, three hundred million dead. No one's entirely certain, what with collateral casualties caused by misuse of biologicals and attempts by belligerents to control Earth's weather systems. The numbers seem to have overwhelmed our record keeping."

"I meant," said Lamoral, "how much did it cost *us*?"

Gloria gave a cold smile of recognition. "You don't change, dear."

"I like to take pride in that."

"The South American vineyards and ranches were hard hit. The facilities at the Matto Grosso spaceport were smashed, but are now rebuilding. The cattle in Montana were lost to plague, bad weather, and military action. The Siberian stock were hard hit by disease, but we saved a breeding population. The plantations in Georgia and South Carolina were converted to food production for the duration of the war, but the first winter cash crops have been seeded. Nothing in Europe suffered direct damage, but the freak weather ruined our wine crop two years running. On the whole, things could have been much worse. We are in decent shape, and our family bank is in good condition to take advantage of reconstruction efforts throughout human space."

"And the family?"

"We're all fine." With asperity. "Thank you for asking."

"I should have been there."

"Yes. We rather think so. We tried to get the Party Set to thaw you, but the person who rejoices in the title of *Queen* Mary Maude Mullen had made a policy decision and gone to sleep for the duration, and no one dared overrule her . . ."

Lamoral's knuckles whitened as he gripped his chair arms. "I'll speak to her about that."

Some inner steel struck Gloria's flinty eyes: sparks flashed. "Sue her and the Set instead. That might attract her attention in a way I could not."

"I'll consider it."

"I think you should visit Regensburg very soon, Lamoral. I've got some new grandchildren you should meet."

"Yes. I agree."

"I will transmit data concerning our financial condition."

"Please do. I'll study it as soon as I can."

Gloria's image winked away. Lamoral found himself staring into the oval mirror, his twin smirking beside him.

"Wait till you hear the *other* news," Alex said. "They woke me up before you, and I've heard some interesting gossip."

"In a moment, Alex. Computer, I have a query."

"At your service." The computer's androgynous voice came from the mirror, and Lamoral had sometimes wondered how many Setmen had asked it in classic rhyme who was the fairest of all, and what the computer had answered. He had not been vain—or unselfconscious—enough to try it himself.

"Please discover the latest whereabouts of Sandrea Salazar Sedillo, former member of the Party Set."

"One moment, please." The computer actually took about three seconds. "Sandrea Salazar and her son, Miguel, are interred at the Holy Faith Crematorium in Aracaju, Sergipe Province, North Brazilian Protectorate. They were cremated on May 3rd, 2140."

Lamoral stared at himself in the mirror. Objectively speaking, he thought, and judging from his appearance, he seemed to have suffered a dreadful psychic blow. He tried to smooth the shock out of his face.

"What was the cause of death?" he asked.

"Exposure to Green Monkey Virus 2140-A, rampant in Brazil at that time."

"Thank you, computer."

"At your service."

Lamoral took a breath, let it out. Back to normal, he thought. "Your gossip, Alex?"

Alex shifted in his seat. "I don't think you want to hear it. Not after that."

"Tell me. I may as well have it all at once."

Alex sighed. "One Set member didn't wake up after the party on Ariel. Cao Cao's said his last ciao-ciao."

"Mm. Dreadful pun. And why should the news upset me?"

"He was murdered. They think you probably did it."

"Ah. Thank you, Alex."

"You asked."

"So I did."

Lamoral contemplated his reflection for another few moments. He rose. "Time to speak to the Doyenne," he said.

* * *

Lamoral had spoken at length to Mary Maude Mullen only once, when he was interviewed for Set membership. Before the interview, he had made inquiries and known what to expect: rows of china dogs, a blazing fire, a peremptory old woman.

Still, on his actual arrival, the concreteness of the study with its endless shelves of porcelain dogs and the enormous fireplace was a bit unsettling, a reminder that from this point on, things were going to grow increasingly unreal. Every single angel is terrible, he thought (quoting Rilke). And this was the abode not of the Angel of Death, but of Life. Which made it more terrifying than anything Rilke had imagined.

The Doyenne, behind her Victorian desk, wore a faintly Edwardian broad-shouldered gown with multiple strands of pearls circling her neck and draping her bosom. With her hair up she looked like Queen Alexandra—either the Russian or the British, take your pick.

A piece of anachronism, he concluded, a part of the self-created legend. Mary Maude had flourished in the Roaring Twenties, one of London's Bright Young Things. Now, with all that over a century away, she was milking her 19th-century birth for everything it was worth. Someone had told Lamoral that she quoted Tennyson as if she'd heard him read idylls in the family parlor.

He studied the pastel dogs. Pinks and greens predominated.

"Do you like my doggies?" she said. Her voice was stronger and far more abrasive than he'd expected.

"They're in ghastly taste," he said, "I assume it's not your own. A useful metaphor, however."

"On your family arms," she said, "there's a dog on a spit."

Lamoral was pleased that he didn't take the bait and glance at the fireplace. "Another metaphor, I suppose," he said. "May I sit down?"

Her glare was colder than the liquid nitrogen that flooded the Set's cold bunkers.

"If you insist," she said.

He took the chair nearest and nudged it closer to the

desk. Heat from the fireplace beat on his profile. He hoped he wasn't about to sweat: that would create the wrong impression entirely.

She was looking at him closely. "Why should someone like Lamoral Johannes Miguel Albert Maria Gabriel, the Inheritor-Prince von Thurn und Taxis, want to join the Party Set?"

Lamoral smiled thinly. "There *is* no one like me, to my knowledge."

"You're a good dancer."

"So I'm told."

"Answer my question."

He was tempted to say, *I just did*. Instead he pretended to give his answer a degree of mature consideration.

"I think the Set would look good on me."

The Doyenne came right back at him. As a boxer, he thought, she'd have a terrific jab. "You evade me, young man. It does you little good."

"Very well." He affected further thought. "I find my family obligations somewhat lacking in challenge. It would be different if I'd actually inherited a country, I suppose, like my cousins the Liechtensteins, but estate and money management palls after a while. I've given up climbing rocks—all the good ones were first climbed long ago, anyway. The Party Set is the sort of thing I'd be doing anyway, only without the advantage of fast-forwarding through the more tedious parts of existence."

"Can you give it up? The family, the traditions, all dozen or so of your castles?"

"All twenty-three, to be precise. And no, I have no intention of giving it all up."

"You'll have to."

"I think not. After all, I'll have to resign and produce an heir at some point."

She fixed her legendary scowl on him. Lamoral avoided being intimidated. "For a member of the Party Set, there *is* no other existence. There is no choice in the matter. Any occupation outside the Set becomes irrelevant—one's family ties crumble away, one's specialized knowledge becomes obsolete, one's occupation ceases to exist."

Lamoral gave her a practiced smile. "I'd like to think of my occupation as timeless."

"You'll see," she said darkly. By which Lamoral took it to mean he'd been accepted.

As he knew he would, even if he'd spent his interview gnawing on human bones. The Party Set, a *nouveau* media aristocracy, would have happily slit a thousand throats for a hint of validation from the *Landadel*, and both he and the Doyenne knew it.

"You'll have to take my brother Alexander as well," he said.

"I hardly think so. More than one member of a family is quite—"

He gave her his most charming smile. "He'll just get into trouble without me to look after him. No, it's both of us, I'm afraid."

And both of them it was. Alex's interview was no less *pro forma* than his own.

He hadn't told the Doyenne that he'd yet to talk Alex into applying, however.

Afterwards, when he and Alex were informed about the Set's custom of presenting gifts to the Doyenne following one's acceptance, they knew at once what to do. The matched set of porcelain dogs were cast in Dresden to careful instructions.

Both china dogs, like those on the Thurn und Taxis arms, were run through with spits, then set in model fireplaces resembling the Doyenne's own.

No sense, thought the two new Set members, in letting anyone forget exactly who was doing favors for whom.

"Mr. von Thurn and, ah—" The stocky black man wore cotton casuals and tennis shoes, but even so his demeanor said *cop*. Lamoral and Alex had encountered him on their way to the Doyenne's office.

"Lamoral. I really don't have a surname."

"Von Thurn and Taxis isn't your name?" The detective's face didn't change expression. So far as Lamoral could tell, the man didn't even blink.

"It's the name of my—forgive me—dynasty. Like the Battenberg-Windsors. They don't have surnames either."

"I see." The expression stayed the same.

"It's very inconvenient, actually." Lamoral decided he might as well spin it out as far as he could, at least till he got some feeling for whether this man was going to do his best to slam him in prison for something he didn't do. "There's really no intermediary degree of formality between 'Lamoral' and 'highness.' " He smiled. "You'll just have to decide how well we're to be acquainted, and use whatever name suits."

The flesh around the man's eyes twitched. He still hadn't managed to blink. "Your highness," he said, "I'm Detective-Superintendent Helmsley of the Bermuda Serious Crimes Unit."

This was going to be difficult, Lamoral decided. The man wasn't easy. "Pleased to meet you," he said. "This is my brother Alexander."

"Why don't you just call us 'Prince,' rather than 'your highness,' " Alex said. "It's quicker."

Helmsley appeared to take this under advisement. "You've heard why I'm here?"

"I believe we have some idea."

"I'd like to ask you both some questions, if I may."

"As you like."

"Miss Mullen has insisted on being present during all questioning. Along with an attorney for the Party Set."

"Very well."

"Prince Lamoral, I think I'd best take you first."

"Certainly, superintendent."

He led him down the humming corridors of the Hall of Sleep, knocked on the door to the Doyenne's office, then opened without waiting for permission. The lower orders, Lamoral thought, had grown cheeky since the dear old Queen's day.

Helmsley hesitated in the doorway, looked at Lamoral and frowned. "Isn't it Mountbatten-Windsor?" he asked.

"They'd like to think so," Lamoral said, entering.

"My brother," explained Alex, "is a traditionalist."

Helmsley closed the door in his face.

Lamoral settled into a chair. He noticed that his dog and Alex's had been set atop the heavy mantelpiece, and assumed this was not because they were the Doyenne's favorites. Perhaps she used them to gauge candidates' reactions.

Perhaps she'd been using them to demonstrate to Helmsley Lamoral's violent and unpredictable state of mind.

After mentioning that the interview was being recorded, Helmsley began his interrogation. Lamoral saw no recorder. All questions concerned who was in the clinic and lounge about the time Cao Cao was getting his prep shot. Helmsley did not concern himself with motives, passions, or relationships. He asked every question several times, phrasing each differently, so as to discover any contradictions. The detective never blinked once. At the end he said thank you, and he and Lamoral rose from their chairs.

"I would like to speak with you after the superintendent talks to Alexander," said the Doyenne.

"And I, you," Lamoral said.

"I will send for you."

Lamoral left the Hall of Sleep and walked out into green, palm-bedecked Bermuda. Set members sat at tables beneath bright umbrellas and sipped drinks that came similarly equipped. Weathered statuary frowned down at them. People frolicked in a salt-water pool with tame dolphins and each other. Several had retained their video shades and were fiddling with them, enhancing Bermuda with technicolor effects. There was a noticeable decrease in the conversational volume as Lamoral stepped onto the verdant lawn. He stepped to the oyster-shaped bar and ordered grapefruit juice.

Carolly approached him. She was wearing a wide-brimmed straw hat over her dark red hair and had perched huge sunglasses on her nose. Her sleeveless sundress was covered with bright splashes of batik.

"Spoken to Helmsley yet?" she asked.

"Yes."

"Did my name come up?"

He sipped grapefruit juice. "Fresh," he said gratefully. "Sweet. Wonderful."

"Thank you for the compliments, dear. But you didn't answer my question."

Lamoral began strolling toward the tables. "Your name arose once or twice."

"I was wondering if he crossed my name off the list of suspects."

"I think mine is still near the top of the list, if that's what you want to know."

Carolly slid her shades farther down her nose. Revealed, her eyes held a speculative cast. "Did you do it, Lamoral?" she asked.

"Do what?"

Carolly frowned. Her shades masked her eyes once more. She and Lamoral arrived at her table. A young woman sat thereat, stunningly attired in a bathing costume in which schools of ambulatory tropical fish, imprisoned somehow beneath its plastic exterior, seemed to provide most of the opaque content. The feat seemed impossible, insofar as the suit itself seemed less thick than the schools of fish swimming inside it.

"I won't ask," Lamoral said.

"Thank you. Answering is getting to be a bore."

"Lamoral," said Carolly, "this is Eurydike Ichimonji-Apostolidis."

Her hair was black as the rings of Uranus. Her eyes were masked by tortoiseshell shades. Lamoral rather approved of the classic lines of her nose. "Pleased to meet you," he said. "Are you a new member of the Set, or tragically some Adjustor or other?"

"The former." Eurydike sipped an exotic rum drink with one hand and twirled its spiral-decorated umbrella with the other.

"Eurydike has done something clever in the sciences," Carolly said, "but I'm afraid I don't understand precisely what."

"I discovered an n-dimensional content to the structure of certain Penrose-tile crystals," Eurydike said. From the way she rattled it off, Lamoral had the impression she'd given this speech a lot in recent days. "This allows access to a hyperdimensional fold within some materials."

"You can hide things inside of other things that wouldn't normally be able to hold them," Lamoral said.

Eurydike nodded. "Very good."

"I have an example," admiring the fish, "right before me."

"Eurydike," Carolly said, "has been a Set member for three days."

"It's been interesting," Eurydike said, "though I hardly expected to find myself in a nest of murderers."

"Rest easy by all means," Carolly said. "We don't kill people until we know them well."

"As long as we're on the subject," Lamoral said, "how was Cao Cao done in, exactly? Helmsley concentrated all his questions on the night of the Uranus party. How can he know it was done then? There've been years in which to stake the man."

"It wasn't a stake, dear." Carolly helped herself to Lamoral's grapefruit juice. "Someone made sure that Cao Cao's prep shot contained nothing but a saline solution."

"Ah. I see."

A twofold problem exists with regard to freezing human tissue: solidifying water expands outward, rupturing cell walls; and those cells that survive undamaged tend to die of oxygen starvation during the warming process. The prep shot solved both difficulties by adding an enzyme that altered the way in which water formed ice crystals, making them more compact and less rigid, and also by providing an amino acid which entered each cell and modified it so as to chemically store oxygen for the long winter.

Lamoral thought about this for a moment. "At least he felt no pain," he said.

Carolly smiled. "I'd prefer to think otherwise. Think about it: every cell in the man's body was squeezed slowly by forming ice crystals. Perhaps his last moments were agony."

"Perhaps."

Eurydike looked from one to the other. "Are all Set conversations so gruesome? I've been hearing nothing but this sort of speculation since Cao Cao failed to rise on schedule yesterday morning."

"Rarely has a Set member been so comprehensively disliked," Carolly explained. "Visualizing his death was an occupation of so many that his shuffling off will doubtless leave many of us with a lot of extra time on our hands.''

"I doubt it," said Lamoral. "All that time and more will be occupied trying to figure out who did it."

Carolly looked uncomfortable. "I'm not looking forward to being the subject of *that* sort of scrutiny." She looked over one shoulder. "I didn't like the way Helmsley looked at me. I have the impression he doesn't care about any of us, doesn't care to know us. Do you suppose he'll settle for just anybody?''

"I expect the Party Set's clout will make him cautious. I did find it disturbing that he doesn't blink, however.''

"Doesn't blink?" Eurydike finished her drink. "He's probably had his eyes replaced with implants, and his inner ears as well. Everything he sees or hears is recorded.''

"Ah. That answers the mystery.''

"One of them, anyway.'' Eurydike rose from her chair. "I'll leave you to continue your necrophilic speculation. I've been listening to this for two days now, and I'm no longer in the mood.''

Lamoral rose with her. "I apologize," he said. "The prospect of death concentrates one's mind wonderfully, to misquote Dr. Johnson, but he neglected to mention that it bores the hell out of everyone else.''

"Some other time, then. After you're no longer a suspect.'' Eurydike stuck out her hand, and Lamoral shook it once, in the French manner. He sat and looked at Carolly, who was watching Eurydike's retreating form.

"Interesting," she said. "Genius plus beauty plus an *n*-dimensional swimsuit. What will they come up with next?''

"Sandy's dead," said Lamoral. "And the boy.''

"I know," Carolly said. There was a silence. Then, "I was trying to think of a way to tell you.''

"I'm sorry Cao Cao's dead.'' Lamoral realized he was speaking with utter sincerity. "It deprives me of the pleasure of doing him in myself.''

Like a cloud drifting over the sun, silence returned and deepened. Lamoral saw Alex wandering out of the Hall of Sleep. The Doyenne was presumably free. Lamoral stood and pushed back his chair.

"Time to confront the dragon," he said.

* * *

"I hope Wayne Unger did it," the dragon said. "That would simplify things. Cao Cao's death would therefore not be the Set's fault; it would be the fault of the authorities who failed to deal with Unger the first time."

"I didn't see Unger outside just now."

"He hasn't been revived yet. His interrogation comes next."

"I wish Helmsley luck getting a coherent story out of him."

Mary Maude Mullen donned a black glove and fed a hefty log into the fire. She had surprising strength, Lamoral observed, for someone of her subjective age. "He won't get much of anything," she said. "People were moving between the clinic, the waiting room, and the cold bunkers continually. Anyone who knew his way around the clinic could have replaced the cartridge of prep solution with a similar cartridge of saline from the cabinets." She turned back to her chair, peeled off the glove. "No," she said. "For a variety of reasons, none of them concerned with the truth, it *needs* to be Unger."

"Unger," said Lamoral, "doesn't have much of a motive."

"He didn't have much of a motive for killing the first time."

"I understood it to be a *crime passionel*."

The Doyenne gave Lamoral a sour look. "Unger has no passions, unless you count his rather pathetic variety of self-loathing. His life might be considered a *search* for passion, if you like." She lowered herself heavily into her chair; her face was set in an expression of distaste. "He didn't kill that silly woman because he loved her, he killed her because he couldn't. He wanted her to fulfill his life by giving it meaning, and it wasn't possible, and the only way the thing could have meaning at all was if he turned it into a tragedy. And of course he failed even at *that*—the laws wouldn't let anyone stay dead, even him."

"That was all a bit before my time." He remembered hearing about the murder, on a radio broadcast, while camped with Alex and Karl-August Hormayr and the others at Olympus Mons Base Camp II. "It gives one occasion," he said, "to wonder about the state of the current laws."

"There have been hundreds of millions killed in a war. People are still dying of various plagues here and there, places where we can't stage Parties for a while. One more death won't be cause for sorrow—if the authorities can find a murderer, they'll kill him."

Lamoral leaned back in his chair and regarded her. "Would that satisfy you?"

"Of course not!" Her look was savage. "The Party Set reflects the world's desire for a perfect, objective guarantor of taste and excellence; and its makeup reflects my own discrimination! A murder within the Set—within *my* Set—casts doubt upon its foundation. *Two* murders and we'll have people saying that the Party Set is nothing but a breeding ground for malignant and violent psychosis!"

"And is it?"

"Don't be absurd!" She slammed a hand on the table. "The entire *world* has just gone through a mass psychosis! The Set is the epitome of sanity by comparison."

Anger rolled in him. He cocked an eye at her. "I slept through that psychosis," he said. "By your order."

"It was the decision of the Board."

"I'm told it was yours."

"The Board chose to act on my analysis."

Lamoral leaned forward, glowering. "I should have spent the war with my family."

There was an expression of malignant triumph on her face. "Set members have no family but the Set."

"That is quite incorrect in my case, as you know. And most of my money is outside the Set, as you also know. I would have wished in such a crisis to make the family decisions necessary—"

"Young man." The Doyenne's tone was peremptory. "I informed you in your first interview that you would have to give it all up. If you chose to think that you could somehow outsmart time, it is no fault of mine. Neither was it my decision where you left your funds. Our Investment Intelligence is perfectly capable—"

"Of losing millions in the Crash of 2130. My own I.I. did very well in that, by the way."

"Any investors have long since been compensated."

"As I hope I will be."

Her eyes flashed again. "For *what*, young man?"

"If I discover that, due to this neglect to consult me on my wishes during the crisis, not to mention the decision not to awaken me on the date of my choice, I or my family have been injured in any way, I and any other injured parties I can locate will bring the Party Set to court for damages. The lawsuit may be lengthy, indeed futile, but the publicity that it, and I, will generate, will be more than you can afford."

Mary Maude Mullen listened to this with an expression of intent calculation. When she spoke it was, to Lamoral's surprise, without hint of malice. "I would not make any more enemies, your serene highness."

"I wasn't aware that I had any."

"I've sat here for the better part of two days listening to the various witnesses describe the events surrounding Cao Cao's demise. It is possible to draw a number of interesting conclusions. It has not occurred to you that Cao Cao may have caught the saline bullet meant for you?"

Lamoral stared at her.

"When you stuck your head in the lounge door with Cao Cao's cigar in your blond mug—" An expression of cold satisfaction trickled across the Doyenne's face. Lamoral assumed the trickle was quite deliberate: for a moment, he loathed her for her enjoyment of this. "—your presence in the prep shot queue was announced to everyone in the room. Anyone could have put the saline cartridge in the hypogun, assuming you'd be next to use it. Cao Cao's arrival, before you finished your cigar, might have been just his bad luck."

Lamoral's mind spun, but he managed to narrow the eddies into a very precise pattern. "And Jameson thought I was Alex . . ."

"And if the murderer couldn't tell you apart from your twin either, then it might have been your brother who was the intended target, yes."

"Who'd kill Alex?" The question had to be asked. "And who'd kill me?"

"I suggest you give the matter some thought." She served up a thin-lipped smile. "I can eliminate certain people from your thoughts. Sandrea Salazar, for example, was never near the clinic that night: she continued the party on Titania and Oberon, in front of many witnesses, before she went to her cold bunker."

"Good."

"And Cao Cao's former associates seem out of the picture. We have investigated our staff, and the crew of the *Queen Mary*, most thoroughly. There isn't a hint of any corruption, and in any case none of them was near the clinic."

"There's Jameson."

"Jameson, my dear, was born two centuries ago. He had no connection with the triads then, and has had little opportunity to form one since. Furthermore, unlike any of the others, he was scarcely out of anyone's sight."

"He could have done it right in front of them. Just taken a cartridge of saline and slotted it into the hypogun. No one would have looked at—at whatever's written on the cartridges. You didn't have to be a member of a triad to dislike Cao Cao."

She beamed at him. Lamoral found the expression a mildly hallucinatory simulacrum of goodwill that was, in its way, terrifying, somewhat like a smile from Tenniel's Duchess. "Very good, my dear," the Doyenne said, "you're beginning to think. Keep it up."

Lamoral gave her an appraising look. "I must say I find it remarkably generous of you, passing on these warnings to someone who just threatened to sue you out of your job."

"It would not do my Party Set the slightest bit of good if you or Alex, or some bystander, were assassinated by whoever it was that killed Cao Cao."

"You know," affecting consideration, "I'm beginning to sympathize with your desire to frame Wayne Unger."

The Doyenne's benevolence faded instantly. Her hand slammed the desk again. "I don't want to frame him! I want the real killer, and I want him out of the Set! I just thought it would be . . . convenient . . . should Unger take the fall."

"You don't think he did it."

"My opinions don't matter."

"You don't think he did it, or we wouldn't be having this conversation."

Her head tilted slightly to one side; her eyes narrowed. It had the appearance of an affectless gesture learned in youth, in 1920s Mayfair or Belgravia; it looked somewhat odd on a would-be Edwardian matron. "Your analysis," she said, "is not altogether without merit."

A kind of joyless mirth bubbled coldly in Lamoral's heart. "You want me to find out who did it."

"You have a good mind, and you are not entirely without resources. You are also motivated by a degree of self-interest. Of course," nodding, "you and your brother could also leave the Set, which would put you safely out of danger."

"Safely out of danger to the Set, anyway."

"A good mind. As I said. Of all my hounds and bitches, you are perhaps the most promising. Pity you never found anything with which to occupy yourself . . ."

Lamoral looked at the fireplace poker and decided that he wanted to take it in hand and smash every china dog in the place. Perhaps, he thought deliberately, he someday would.

"I want to know why Cao Cao was admitted to the Set," he said.

"He was charming, wealthy, polite." This was too glib, Lamoral thought. "He was an interesting man, an inventor."

"Tell me the real reason, Doyenne. His background alone made him unsuitable, and you know it."

She scowled, an expression far less frightening than her smile. "He had a lot of stock in the Party Set."

"So have others who've never got in."

Mary Maude Mullen gave a sigh. "Our I.I. was totally outfoxed during the Crash of 2130. Our finances were . . . tottering. Cao Cao's financial resources were enormous. It's one of the world's great fortunes."

"He bailed you out."

"Exactly." She looked grim. "It won't happen again. It was the one exception I've made in all these decades, and this disgrace has resulted."

A bell gently chimed. Mary Maude Mullen lifted her chin. "Yes, computer."

"Doyenne, Mr. Unger has been awakened. Superintendent Helmsley wishes to interrogate him as soon as possible."

"Tell him he may come at any time. Inform the legal staff as well."

"As you wish, Doyenne."

Lamoral rose. "I'll give this all due thought, Miss Mullen."

"I hope you will."

Lamoral had one thought already fixed in mind. He headed for the comm link.

"How's our liquidity?" Lamoral asked.

Gloria considered it. "Not as bad as it once was. We have enough capital for the odd venture or two."

"I was thinking of acquiring more Party Set stock."

"It's a solid investment. But we already have a substantial bloc in our portfolio."

"But not a controlling interest."

Gloria's eyes glittered. "I see."

"Have we the funds available?"

"No. Of course not. We would need partners."

Lamoral gave it some thought. "The time hasn't come to go public with the scheme, not even discreetly. But let us buy stock, yes. Through the bank, our companies, the family . . . as many blinds as possible."

"Very well."

"The price will drop shortly, if it hasn't already. Certainly within twenty-four hours."

"Yes?" Gloria was interested.

"I don't have time right now to explain why. But have the I.I. monitor the stock. You'll know when to buy."

"This scheme won't be easy."

Lamoral looked at her and gave her a tiger smile. "I have all the time I need, don't I?"

"I hope I live to see it, Lamoral. That queen bitch dethroned."

"And her pack of dogs with her."

Gloria seemed bemused. "You shall have to explain that remark to me some time, Lamoral."

"I will. In Regensburg."

"You're coming soon? I'll tell the family."

"At the very least," laughing, "we'll make a lot of money."

"Never," said Gloria, "is that a small consideration."

Lamoral found the rest of the Party Set in the auditorium going through part of their Adjustment, in this case a video bringing them up to date on contemporary history.

The Set was not a good audience for this sort of fare. They chatted, laughed, moved from seat to seat. The Adjustors, having no choice, put up with it all, but broadcast their scowling disapproval from the lectern. Lamoral found Carolly sitting next to Eurydike and joined them.

"What have I missed?" Lamoral asked.

Carolly looked at her watch. "About the first fifty million casualties."

Soldiers exploded from shuttles in jittery verité images. Projectiles chopped chunks out of concrete and, occasionally, people. The Matto Grosso spaceport, in the background, was burning.

Lamoral looked at the carnage with interest. "I believe my family's about to lose a substantial investment. I hope to hell we're insured."

Rockets hammered concrete. A landing web toppled.

"And to think," said Eurydike, "that we slept through it all."

Lamoral looked at her. Her eyes, uncovered by sunglasses, had a pleasant Eurasian tilt. The startling bathing suit had gone: she was wearing a simple cotton shift. "You slept through it?" Lamoral asked. "I thought you'd only joined the Set a few days ago."

"I saw what was coming. When it looked as if things were going to oscillate out of control, I retired to my own cold bunker in the Apostolidis complex in Mexico City."

"Sensible of you."

"Events were cascading into a nonlinear instability pattern

of classic dimensions. You could chart it with a Lorenz equation if you wanted.''

''And didn't someone? Wouldn't that have provided a warning?''

She shrugged and gave him a weak smile. ''Who listens to mathematicians?''

''Ah.''

''Events were too complex. None of the major powers in space wanted to fight: they were all dragged into it by their allies, here on Earth and elsewhere. Whenever the space powers settled things between themselves, their allies would start fighting in some backwater like Canada or Ceres, settling old scores, and the powers got dragged back in again.''

''Like the First World War.''

''More like the Pelopponesian. World War I was pretty linear once it got going. The Pelopponesian—seen as mathematics, it was entirely nonlinear. Chaos. The big winner was Persia, which didn't even do any fighting.''

''And who's the winner here?''

''Radical technologies, probably. By the end, every technology held back by our peaceful, conservative order got deployed by the powers.''

''And those technologies are?''

''I bet this video won't tell us. It seems pretty superficial to me.''

''Good God,'' said Carolly. ''Was that the Kremlin?''

Lamoral looked up at the screen. ''Built of wood, unfortunately.''

''I hope they got some of the treasures out.''

They watched until the images from Russia were replaced with the sight of robot hunter-killer tank units storming across the Gobi in vast clouds of dust. The strange thing was that they appeared literally from nowhere, from out of a barnlike structure, like a host of clowns from out of a midget car.

Lamoral stared. ''Did you do that?'' he asked Eurydike.

Her expression was stolid. ''I'm afraid I did.''

Carolly seemed puzzled. ''If you can hide the contents of an aquarium in a bathing suit,'' Lamoral explained, ''imagine what you can do with a house and an armored brigade.''

Carolly was impressed.

"I've changed my mind," Eurydike said. "The big winner in this war was the Party Set."

"How so?" asked Carolly.

"We missed it all. In a war, that's the definition of victor."

After the history lesson came a fashion show. The Party Set watched this part of Adjustment with rather more attention. Lamoral strolled toward Alex and sat down next to him.

"We have a problem," he said.

"Yes?"

Lamoral told him. Alex listened with a mildly amused expression. Lamoral finished, and Alex gave a little frown as he watched a mannequin bounce down the runway in a zoot suit with lapels as wide as the shoulders and the pleated trousers pegged up to the armpits. "You're not going to put that jacket on *me*," Alex said.

"I suspect you're not being given a chance in the matter."

Alex sighed. "Do you really think it's true? Or was it the Doyenne trying to get a bit of revenge?"

"I don't know. I've been too surprised by the idea to give it much rational thought."

"Besides—who'd kill you, Lamoral? I can't think of a soul."

"I wish I could say the same for you, Alex."

Alex affected surprise. "You mean Edwardes? The business with Helen Nomathemba was *years* ago."

"The Party Set," Lamoral said, "necessarily has somewhat flexible attitudes with regard to time. He did challenge you to a duel, for god's sake, and duelling's *centuries* out of fashion."

Lamoral's eyes drifted to Thomas Edwardes, who sat in the last row of the auditorium where he could gaze down at everyone, brooding above the entire Party Set. He looked as if he had a lot to brood about. Maybe he was working up to another murderous aria.

"But really," Alex protested. "It's too absurd."

"*Ora e per sempre addio* . . . He sang it with great conviction."

"I thought his voice was very clearly not what it was. All

his conviction came from Lilt.'' Alex shifted uncomfortably in his seat. ''Kill me over a woman? Ridiculous.''

''She left the Set after you left her.''

''The *last* murder in the Set was over a woman. Edwardes would never be so unfashionable as to provide Unger with a chorus. He'd demand his own aria, at least.''

''As I recall, he sang it.''

''Pish.'' There was another man on the runway. His suit was silver mesh and had fins on the shoulders. There was a lightning bolt on his chest and a cowl that masked the upper half of his face.

''If we're going to start talking about affairs of the heart,'' Alex said, ''you're just as guilty as I am.''

''I didn't seduce Edwardes' girlfriend away from him.''

''What about Carolly? You and she have a history.''

''We've remained the best of friends.''

''Why did she join the Set, Lamoral?''

''The usual reason, I suppose. It happened well before my time.''

''That's part of my point. She was a very well-known actress, you know. But when actresses get to a certain age, parts get harder to find.''

Lamoral was annoyed. ''Are you serious about this?''

''And then you took up with her protégée, a much younger woman. D'you think Carolly isn't sensitive about things like that?''

Lamoral regarded his brother coldly. ''You are growing offensive, Alex.''

''Sorry.'' Alex's expression was smug. ''But I'm just proposing a scenario that's just as likely as . . .''

''It's not likely at all.''

''Stop turning royal on me. I think the Doyenne's done this deliberately. I think she's trying to keep us from . . . well, from thinking about what we'd otherwise be thinking about.''

''If that's what she's trying to do,'' Lamoral said, ''she hasn't succeeded.''

''I'm pleased.''

The superhero walked off, replaced by a woman who came out dressed as a cartoon mouse, with round ears and big yellow shoes. Some of the audience tittered.

"If the Set tries to get me to wear any of this," Alex said, "I'm going to sleep till the next war."

"I think the Set is going to be a big hit in the next decade or so," Lamoral said. "Fantasy is obviously going to be very popular following the years of war."

"Provided, of course, we don't start imitating the outside and slaughtering each other. Our ratings would drop for sure."

Lamoral couldn't tell if Alex was being serious or not.

On reflection, Lamoral considered, he'd always had that problem.

"Am I mistaken," said Kitsune Takami, "or does the waiter have an extra pair of arms?"

"It would appear so," said Lamoral.

"If it's a disability, I suppose I should ignore it, or offer my sympathies," Kitsune said. "But suppose he had it *done* and expects compliments?"

Lamoral inspected the waiter at a distance. He hulked above the Set members, taller than most, wide as a beer truck. His bald head, with its flattened features, looked less a human feature than a grotesque helmet. "Considering his size and fierce mien," Lamoral said, "I wouldn't care to make the wrong choice."

"Exactly."

The Party Set was going through the usual post-Adjustment dance. Bermuda was virtually under siege: politicians and celebrities were fully prepared to cut one another's throats for an invitation to the first Set function in six years, even though none of the Adjustment activities was supposed to be recorded and the dance was, as far as Set functions went, strictly off the record.

"Dance?" Lamoral offered.

"Of course." She smiled. "They'll think we're murderers conspiring together."

Kitsune's ball gown consisted of a single strap, about three inches broad and black in color, wound carefully about her lanky body. She was in glass heels that made her even taller. Glitter dusted her cheekbones and shoulders. Lamoral, classically formal in his dinner jacket, was uncertain where it was safe to place his hands.

"Don't worry," Kitsune said. "It won't shift."

"I'll take your word for it."

The music was slow and soothing, intended as a complement to a perfect Bermuda evening. Steel drums plonked off the deliberately-corroded marble façade of the pseudo-Roman amphitheater. Lamoral noticed that some of the orchestra were playing more than one instrument, with more than one set of arms.

"I think compliments are in order for the waiter. Sporting an extra pair of arms seems to be a coming fashion."

"I think I'll pass on that one. I get enough stares on account of my height."

Kitsune's evening strap seemed not to be shifting. Lamoral could feel the warmth and texture of her skin through it. He offered his congratulations.

"Some new miracle adhesive. Developed in the war."

"Isn't it painful when you remove it?"

"There's a solvent. It'll also dissolve on its own, in a few hours, in case I forgot to bring my little spray bottle."

"Leaving you like a kind of reverse Cinderella. In glass slippers and nothing else."

Kitsune seemed amused. "I imagine the designer must have had something like that in mind."

"Do you have a similar costume for the Day of the Dead?"

"I don't think I'll be attending. It might be considered bad taste, with the war and all."

"I'd like to see what the world is like. Six years was too long to be so completely out of touch."

"The world is the same as it was, only worse. I can't say I'm intrigued."

The dance came to an end. Lamoral escorted Kitsune off the floor. Waiting on the fringes was a ranked host of guests—the "normal" people the Set were supposed to mix with as part of Adjustment—all lurking in ambush for the next dance with Kitsune. "The dance ended before I could ask you about Liu Shuyuan," he said.

"It doesn't matter anymore, does it?"

"I suppose not. But we were going to be murderers conspiring, weren't we?"

"True." She hesitated on the fringe of the dance floor. A man in the front of the pack—Lamoral recognized the President of the Bank of Bermuda—took a hesitant step forward, then back. Then gave a self-conscious Lilting laugh.

"Was Liu the man who developed Lilt?" Lamoral asked.

Kitsune shook her head. "No. That rumor proved not to be true, or at least not true in its more sensational dimensions. The man you mean was Carlos Vandermeer. He and Cao Cao worked together, Vandermeer under contract, and rather than bump him off as per legend, Cao Cao gave him a small fortune and set him up in a perfectly legitimate business in Bali, where he prospered and lived happily ever after."

"Another legend shattered."

The band began to play. The bank president made another hesitant little shuffle.

"Liu was a genuine skeleton in Cao Cao's closet," Kitsune said. "He was Cao Cao's maternal uncle. When the family relocated to L4, he got left behind and, uh, snuffed."

"Is that all?"

"They could have saved him."

The pack, led by the bank president, was inching closer. Lamoral gave them a sympathetic look requesting patience.

"You see," Kitsune said, "they left him behind deliberately, and they put the word out he was responsible for a lot of the family's decisions. The triads got their pound of flesh that way. And when you consider how people in that part of the world feel about family loyalty, you can see it would be a major source of embarrassment to Cao Cao to have all this known, yes?"

"I see."

"I had more information, don't worry. A veritable banquet. Liu was just the first appetizer." She sighed. "Pity I won't get to serve up the full meal."

"You'll have to tell me dessert sometime."

"Certainly. Perhaps the best analogous dessert would be chocolate death, *n'est-ce pas*?"

With a gesture, Lamoral relinquished Kitsune to the mob.

"Thank you," he said, stepping out of the way to avoid getting trodden on. "I'll look forward to the banquet, even if it's a vicarious one."

She nodded and surrendered herself to the bank president. Lamoral shortly found himself dancing with a self-conscious deb whose awkwardness was compensated by a very nice smile, at least once he got her smiling. After the dance he escorted her to the bar and left her with a drink and its tiny batik parasol. Heading back, he noticed Wayne Unger on his way to the bar. Unger saw the four-armed waiter nearby, closer than the bar, at which point Unger lurched for the drink tray and helped himself to a pair of martinis.

"Careful, Unger," Lamoral said, approaching. "You haven't got the new liver yet."

Unger was watching the waiter's receding back. "It can't be the DTs. I've barely started."

"My last dance partner informed me," Lamoral said, "that what you're looking at is a genuine space commando. The extra arms are to assist with warfare in the weightless dimension."

Unger gave a shudder, then quaffed the first martini. He looked around for someplace to set the empty glass, saw none, and amiably chucked the glass toward a replica of an Easter Island statue. It bounced off the statue's tiny torso and rolled on the grass.

"He's only a few years old," Lamoral went on. "Grew up in a tank and got force-fed his education via electrode. Now the war's over the few surviving warriors have been demobbed and set free to search for gainful employment."

"Mighty broadminded of the Party Set to hire him," Unger said. "I had always hoped that, when human modification came, it would be for purposes aesthetic rather than military. Instead—" He gestured with his martini at the waiter's broad back. "What rough beast."

"Ein jeder Engel ist schrecklich."

Unger seemed momentarily startled. "I'd forgotten—that was dedicated to an ancestor of yours, wasn't it?"

Lamoral looked at the waiter's receding back. "I bet he'd like to throttle the lot of us."

"It's an impulse that comes over everyone on occasion."

"I take it, by the fact you're here at all, that you've been cleared by Detective Helmsley."

"Insofar as anyone's been cleared." Unger gave a shrug and finished his second martini. The glass s̶ ̶ ̶ ̶ ̶d in the eye of the stone Long-ear.

"Did you do it?"

Unger grinned. "Let's get another drink."

They headed for the bar, and Unger got two more martinis. Lamoral had some prewar Bernkastel out of a bottle with one of his chateaus on it. It hadn't aged well.

Unger waved a glass at the crowd, the four-armed warriors and the pack of sweaty celebrities. "The time grows nigh," he said. "Signs are all about us. The beasts and the angels surround us and deafen us with their barking. Soon the peace of Ariel will descend."

"That's what you want?"

"A curtain of black snow." Unger slammed down the first drink, swayed, placed the glass on the bar with an odd delicacy of movement. "I wanted to see the finish, I guess. That's why I'm here." He belched. "To look right in the pathetic eyes of the last pale, wormy, pathetic denizen of this corroded old planet and remind him what *promise* we once had. Then lie down in the black snow and close my eyes and pursue the final liberty, as your family's tame poet put it, not to interpret roses."

" 'O trees of life, when will your winter come?' "

Unger looked severe. "Don't mix elegies. It shows your erudition, but demonstrates a disturbing lack of narrative sense."

"My apologies."

Another belch came. "I'm working on something new. I hope I will be able to recite it soon."

"Good."

"I believe I must vomit now."

"Do get that new liver, won't you?"

"Whatever needs doing." Spoken vaguely as Unger headed for a patch of friendly earth.

Lamoral turned to the dance floor and shared a set with an Italian actress who expected to be recognized and was offended when she was not; a desperate wannabee who talked endlessly about her analysis, as if that somehow made her interesting; and a terrified Somebody's Daughter who didn't want to be here. He was glad to sit out the next dance, and found himself standing next to Helmsley.

The detective was still in his baggy cottons and tennis shoes. His unwinking eyes scanned the crowd incessantly. Lamoral gave him a smile. "Any luck, superintendent?"

Helmsley's face turned toward Lamoral but resolutely resisted any temptation to change expression. "I've interrogated everyone concerned. There's no way of proving anything."

"But you have your suspicions."

"I can't prove suspicions. The murder happened six years ago and two billion kilometers outside my jurisdiction. There's no physical evidence, and everyone had opportunity. I can hope for an eventual confession, but since it's the Party Set the confession will probably happen centuries after I'm dead." His robot eyes turned back to the crowd. "I suppose I can live with the suspense."

"I'm curious. None of your questions pertained to motive."

"Motive isn't provable either. Our prosecutors and judges have computer assistants who prefer physical evidence."

"I see."

"I wouldn't hold my breath for that confession. Whoever did it is a born killer."

Lamoral looked at him. "Indeed?"

"I was recording, remember? In great detail. Pulse and breath rates, involuntary eye movement, pupil dilation, blush response—you'd be amazed what can be done with blush response."

"Physical evidence for your computers?"

"Yes." The implanted eyes turned to Lamoral. "The killer's a sociopath. The murder didn't disturb him at all, no more than pulling up a weed. He or she showed no sign of stress or abnormality—just breezed through the interrogation because there was no internal conviction that anything wrong had been done."

A cold, queasy feeling settled into Lamoral's being. He really didn't want to know any of this.

"Perhaps," he said, "you haven't interrogated the right person."

"Do you believe that?"

Lamoral said nothing.

"Didn't think so," Helmsley said. "I think I should tell you that you and your brother ought to hope that it was really Cao Cao the killer was after."

Lamoral gave an uneasy smile and shrugged. "Who'd kill *me*?" he said.

A shrug. "If you don't know, I don't."

"I think I should ask someone to dance."

"Don't let me stop you."

"I thank you for your warning."

"You're welcome." The artificial eyes flicked toward Lamoral. "Try not to get killed in my jurisdiction. I'd hate to go through all this futility again."

"I'll do my very best to oblige, superintendent."

"Good luck."

Lamoral thought the wish simply good form on the detective's part. The Party Set was a distant cinema fantasy moving through his present; it wasn't as if he cared about them, or they for him.

That kind of thing, given the realities, just wasn't possible.

Not many of the Set attended El Día de los Muertos. The war and Cao Cao's murder raised, some said, serious questions of taste concerning a festival that celebrated death. Alex, Kitsune, and Carolly announced their intentions of sleeping through it. Lamoral brooded about their reasons: perhaps they just wanted to avoid a celebration of something the entire Party Set was created in order to deny.

Lamoral went alone, dropping onto the landing field in his two-seater Hirondel, and hoped to find in the celebration of mortality some kind of focus for his thoughts.

But he hadn't expected the fiesta to take place on a battlefield. Guadalajara had been fought over, and afterward an earthquake had perpetrated a Brownian redistribution of the rubble. The Day of the Dead was held in front of what had been the colonial governor's palace, a building as classical, and as dead, as the Party Set's phony Roman ruins. Long

strands of particolored lights had been strung up around the
plaza, each bright bulb alternating with a grinning skeleton
that danced in the fitful wind. VTOs dropped from the sky
in graceful silence, disgorging a cheerful and macabre crowd.
Surrounding the cleared area was a circle of police, and beyond it more lights: the fires of those who lived outside the
enchanted circle.

Too many of the celebrants, Lamoral thought, had come
dressed as soldiers, their faces painted to resemble skulls.

He was himself in a red satin cavalier's outfit, suitable for
Poe's *Masque* as well as this one. He'd ordered it for the
festival six years ago, and it had waited in his closet ever
since.

The Virgin of Zapopan, a miraculous survivor of the
bombing, took a tour of the ruins, riding with the bishop in
an open-topped Tin Lizzie. Folk dancers pirouetted in
flounced skirts. The cadet band from Chapultepec, garbed in
Napoleonic splendor, bounced brassy notes off the torn corners of buildings. After Taps, the party began in earnest.

Eurydike Ichimonji-Apostolidis approached Lamoral atop
the guest grandstand and mutely offered ceviche on a tortilla
chip. Lamoral ate it.

"Too much parsley."

"I thought so, too."

She wore a long gown on which—in which?—skeletons,
attired in tie and tails, tap-danced with bamboo canes
clutched in segmented white fingers. Their moves, Lamoral
observed, were really very good.

"Are the skeletons from the same quarter as the fish?"
Lamoral asked.

"No. These aren't hiding in the nth dimension, they're a
video projection. They're programmed to follow the Astaire
solos from several of his films."

"You're wearing a TV set?"

"More or less."

"Are you also recording?"

She shook her head. "Not I."

Lamoral helped himself to more ceviche from a bowl she
was carrying. "I'd ask you to dance," he said, "but I'm
afraid your skeletons would show me up."

"That's all right. My uncle Guzmán has the first dance anyway."

"Any relation of the president?"

"His nephew. A senator."

Lamoral looked at her. "Did you grow up in Mexico? You seem to have done more here than spend six years in a cold bunker."

She grinned. "I didn't grow up in any one place or another, but I spent a lot of time in Mexico, yes. I love it."

"I suppose that would explain your presence at this event."

Eyebrows lifted. "Shouldn't I be here? This is the first Party Set event since I've joined."

"Yesterday you found our conversation morbid, and this fiesta, after all, celebrates morbidity."

Mariachis called out from the bandstand, an explosion of trumpets. Eurydike laughed at the sound.

"I used to come here when I was little. The skeletons were all my friends."

"I should like to hear about your childhood sometime."

"We would seem to have all the time necessary." She saw her uncle Guzmán, waved, and danced away on feet as light as those of the dead Astaires.

Outside the perimeter, the lights flickered and heaved. The crowd trying to get a better view of things.

"Ah. Lamoral." A heavy hand clapped Lamoral's shoulder. Lamoral turned and saw that the hand was Edwardes'. Lamoral made a note to the effect that Edwardes could tell him from his brother, even from behind and in a disguise. Probably the killer had wanted Cao Cao after all.

The tenor was dressed as the Reaper himself, his visage hooded by a monk's cowl, a rosary wound round his waist.

"Lamoral. We want you to hear something," Edwardes said. His face had a twitchy Lilt smile. Unger lurched into view from behind Edwardes' towering form. Sweat was ruining the poet's fine skull makeup. A garland of roses embraced his forehead.

"Isn't that painful?" Lamoral asked.

"Poets learn to enjoy the thorns. Listen."

"At last his unromantic heart
Was broken, the only way
Possible, pierced from
Within by perfect sextile spears.

Was it not absolute already, that
Sub-zero manner, the cold ammonia
That lisped from his mantis tongue?
He came among us
A faultless monument to frost.

The final deperition
Followed by years the
Triumph of the metaphor.
His prescient cenotaph, already built,
Points his dying-place—the gutter X
Filled with upwelling rubble, all cold;
A horizon of black; and poison drifts
Of implacable, maculate snow."

"We're thinking of having it set to music," Edwardes said. "I'll sing it at my Christmas concert."

"It's good," said Lamoral, "but it'll never replace 'Jingle Bells.' "

Edwardes gave a long, delighted giggle, all Lilt. "That's good, Unger." He nudged the poet with an elbow. "Jingle bells!" he said.

Lamoral looked at Unger. "I almost wish you hadn't made the effort," he said. "I wish you'd memorialized Sandy instead."

There was a moment of silence. "I think it's been done," Unger said. "By people more talented than myself."

There was a bad taste in Lamoral's mouth. "As the Muse moves you, Unger."

"I'll do it!" cried Edwardes.

He tossed his monk's cowl back with a quick, wired gesture, and suddenly the glorious voice spread its wings over the plaza.

"Tu che a dio spiegasti l'ali . . ."

Edwardes' voice rolled like a great wave over mariachi brass. Lamoral watched with cold incredulity as Edwardes lamented the passing of Lucia di Lammermoor, and he tried to decide whether Sandy would have liked it this way, an improvised memorial in the midst of the dancing dead, a sobbing tenor in combat with brassy dance music . . . He decided she probably would have liked it, if her mood was in the right place, but that ultimately it didn't matter. All the shades were here tonight, emissaries from the grave, from the future, their identities concealed behind skull-masks and gaiety . . .

Behind him a woman was weeping. Tears spilled out of the eyeholes of her mask. Tears fell down Edwardes' face in accompaniment.

There was a ripple of shots, of explosions. A bright, smoky form moved on balloon tires across the plaza, the *Totentanz* all done in fireworks, Death hand in hand with dancing mortals, types created in broad caricature: peasant, worker, capitalist, soldier. This was where proletarian art survived, Lamoral thought, in Mexican firework *castillos*. People shouted and applauded. Death's grin winked briefly off the polished skin of a descending Dart. Outside the perimeter, lights massed in other, fleeting patterns. Lamoral could see police shifting position.

Edgardo perished by his own hand—Edwardes actually sagged to the ground—and Lucia went into the tomb. Lamoral thanked moist-eyed Edwardes for the memorial and stepped off the grandstand into the mass of people. Skulls grinned at him from all sides. A second *castillo* went off: sharp detonations revealed Poe with a raven on his shoulder, another ghost visiting the proceedings. The crowd roared its welcome. There was a hysteria in the sound that Lamoral didn't like.

A surge almost took him off his feet. He found a safe eddy in the mass and caught his breath. A vision in white lace caught his eye, a skeleton in the form of a bride, walking arm-in-arm with a dapper Asian man.

Lamoral's heart hammered. He stared, but the vision had turned away.

Angels (says Rilke) are often unable to tell whether they move among the living or the dead.

Lamoral shouldered through the charnel mass, keeping the bride's high white comb in sight. *Castillos* burst into crackling fire. Angels and demons battled each other across the sky. There was a scream, the sight of descending fists. Lamoral fought his way through the crowd.

Unger had his arms around Edwardes' huge torso, trying to drag him off the struggling form of Cao Cao, who was fighting gamely but was smothered by Edwardes' bulk. Edwardes' massive black hands were tightened around Cao Cao's throat. The death-bride's long veil was askew; she screamed and beat on Edwardes' shoulders with her fists. *Castillos* burst into raucous life. Lamoral rushed forward in a crouch, slammed a shoulder into Edwardes' chest, drove him back. Unger, driven back as well, stumbled and fell. Edwardes tripped over him and crashed massively to the cobbles.

Alex rose from the rubble and tore off his Cao Cao mask. Indira Batish dashed to his aid, her bridal costume giving a long rip as someone stepped on it. Edwardes roared up from Unger's embrace and Lamoral kicked the tenor in the face, dropping him atop Unger again. Alex's eyes started from his head as he tried to scrape Edwardes' paw prints off his throat.

Shots echoed over the plaza. There were screams and the crowd surged.

"They've broken through!" someone shouted.

"It was a *joke*, you idiot!" Alex yelled. He had the beginnings of a terrific shiner.

A wall of panicked skeletons stumbled over Unger and Edwardes, burying them. Lamoral was driven away from them all: he could hear Indira's scream of outrage as she was torn away from Alex. Shots crackled out. Lamoral realized it wasn't fireworks anymore. He ran for his VTO, but everyone else had the same idea, and the mob swarmed into the tight confines of the parking field, so tightly that no one could move, and no rocket could rise.

A preprogrammed *castillo* filled the sky with gargoyles built of garish light. In the blazing red and green Lamoral saw skeletons staggering in the press with uncanny grace; he fought his way to Eurydike, lashed with elbows to make room and air for them both. Gunshots flogged the air. Half the people were sobbing, the other half screamed in anger. There was another volley and suddenly the crowd was running in a different direction. The way to the VTO was clear.

The hatch opened to Lamoral's handprint. The interior of the two-seater Hirondel had the reassuring smell of fine leather. Eurydike wept against Lamoral's shoulder as he told the machine to take them to Regensburg.

"There are personnel within range of the boosters," the Hirondel reported. "I am warning them to stand clear."

Skeletons danced in graceful pirouette. The hull rang to faint volleys. "As soon as possible, computer," Lamoral said. He found Eurydike's lips and kissed them.

"Lifting now," said the computer.

"To the palace, and quickly," Lamoral said, as if the computer could whip up the coach horses. He found Eurydike's lips again.

The scattered dead dropped away beneath them.

Eurydike reclined on a pile of pillows and finished her glass of Marcobrunn. "My uncle Guzmán warned me something might happen," she said. "The government's been trying to get the squatters out of the ruins so they can rebuild."

"The government wanted the squatters to crash in?" Lamoral asked. "They provoked it?"

"Not *all* the government. Not the Guzmán faction. But Guadalajara's mayor and ruling clique, yes."

"Huh. Just *let* them try to get another Set function within the next century."

"Small comfort."

"My personal consolation," said Lamoral, "is that I'm going to outlive the lot of them by centuries."

Eurydike gave a small smile. "There is that. Yes." She looked at him curiously. "What was that business with the book last night? Stepping in, then out, then in again?"

"A sort of a ritual. Don't trouble yourself over it."

It was early evening in Bavaria. Things had been sorted out in Mexico: no Set members had perished, and Alex, Edwardes, and Indira were bunkered down back in Bermuda. Wayne Unger was getting his new liver in a clinic in Morocco.

There was a knock on the door. Eurydike drew a sheet

over herself while Lamoral reached for the gold door-handle
and opened it. A servant in livery, complete with silk stock-
ings and knee breeches, offered a package.

"For the lady, your serene highness."

"Thank you." Lamoral took the package and closed the
door. He put it on the marble surface of the 17th-century
dressing table and turned to Eurydike.

"We'll be dining with my family. I took the liberty of
ordering suitable clothing."

"Will they fit?"

"Of course. I called Bermuda for your measurements, and
my sister's dressmaker whipped up something appropriate
while you were asleep."

Eurydike laughed. "You got all this done after I drifted
off? Don't you ever sleep?"

"For years at a time."

"Right. I forgot." She laughed again. Lamoral decided he
liked the sound.

Eurydike waved an arm, indicating the room with its white
and gold rococo molding, the floating nymphs and cherubs
cavorting across the domed ceiling, the half-acre of canopied
bed, the crusted porcelain vases and gleaming antique
furniture, the Poussin landscape over the gilt porcelain fireplace . . .

"Joining the Party Set can't have been much of a change
for you, could it? You were living in a fantasy world already."

"Without the benefits of Adjustment."

She leaned forward. "So why'd you do it?"

"Join the Set, you mean?"

"If you can afford servants in knee breeches instead of
robots, you can afford your own cold bunkers. You could
have your own damn Set, and your taste's probably better
than the Doyenne's anyway. So why did you need Mary
Maude Mullen and company?"

Lamoral stepped to the silver Flaxman ice pail and withdrew a half-empty bottle of Marcobrunn. Ice clinked cheerfully in the pail's interior.

"Another glass?"

"Yes. And my question answered, please."

Lamoral poured. "If you promise not to spread it about."

"Cross my heart and hope to be embarrassed in some horrible public fashion."

They clinked glasses. Lamoral sat on the bed and leaned against the carved ivory-inlaid bedpost. "During the Bolshevik Interregnum the family lost our property in Hungary, Prussia, and Bohemia. A dozen or so castles, of which only Chraustowitz and Chotieschau were really worth getting upset about, but there was a lot of land attached."

"But these were returned, yes?"

"Most of it. After the family bank made certain loans to the governments concerned, yes."

"Ah."

"Anyway, there was still the problem of inheritance taxes, which remained rather stiff over there. While my grandfather was the current prince, my father renounced the inheritance in order to avoid passing property to me crippled by more than one tax assessment—he took minor holy orders and retired to Neresheim Abbey, which is one of the family churches, quite the nicest one by the way—and that made me Inheritor-Prince."

"I see where this is heading," Eurydike said, "and I'm not quite sure I believe it."

"To quote a friend of mine quoting someone she could never quite remember, you can look it up."

"I will. Believe me."

"So I joined the Set, and I'll live for centuries. My grandfather's death put quite a dent in the family finances, but the dent should be well hammered out by the time I have an heir and breathe my last—"

"You joined the Set to avoid paying inheritance taxes!" Eurydike was delighted.

"One shouldn't pay them, you know." Sipping Marcobrunn. "Not more than once a century, anyway."

"It's got to be the greatest tax dodge in history!"

"It isn't as if I haven't been having a good time."

"I can see you have."

"You should dress. My sister will want to give us supper, and I'll give you the short tour on our way to the dining room."

"The short tour?"

"Schloss St. Emmeram has over 500 rooms."

"Good grief. Are they all furnished like this one?"

"More or less. The offices in the old medieval wing tend to be more functional." Lamoral refilled his glass and walked to the door. "I'll be in the hall outside," he said.

"Lamoral?"

He put his palm on the door-handle, turned to face her. "Yes?"

Eurydike looked at him intently. "How did your family get all this in the first place?"

Lamoral smiled. "We invented the science of modern data management and transmission."

"You owned IBM or something?"

"Not quite. We ran the first post office."

"Oh." Eurydike blinked. "You moved hardcopy."

"Hardcopy," Lamoral said, "was big in those days. We had the mail monopoly for the Holy Roman Empire, and pretty much moved hardcopy for everyone else in Europe and Latin America as well."

Eurydike thought about it. "I guess hardcopy was the thing, all right."

Lamoral stepped into the hallway and closed the door behind him.

Schloss St. Emmeram, stone and marble and plaster and gilt, loomed in vast, serene silence around him.

Hardcopy.

Footsteps echoed in the grand ballroom. Endless reflections marched casually through mirrored walls. The place, all silver and white, was huge: whole teams of horses could have danced in it. Far above, the massive crystal chandeliers chimed faintly to the sound of Lamoral's words.

"St. Emmeram started out as a gothic monastery. But when the family bought the place and moved here in the 19th Century, they built a new wing that tripled the size of the place. That's where we are now."

Eurydike seemed a little dazed by it all, particularly after she'd met a jolly little man named Otto, whose sole occupation was to progress from room to room and wind all the clocks . . . The problem of scale was getting to her, as well it might.

"Here's the throne room." Lamoral threw open a set of doors.

Eurydike stepped inside. The throne room was fairly small, at least considering the scale of the rest of the schloss; and the throne itself, gilt and red cushions, scarcely inspired awe, especially as it was dwarfed by a towering canopy. Eurydike approached the dais and gave the chair a look.

"You were crowned on this?"

"Afraid not," Lamoral said. "It's not for us. No one in the family's ever sat on it, or anyway admitted to it. See, we used to represent the Habsburg emperors at the Everlasting Diet, and the throne's supposed to be for them. But since the Diet had already proved less than everlasting by the time the throne room was even built, and the lady who built it was a bit dotty on the subject of Habsburgs, one begins to wonder."

Eurydike raised an eyebrow. "I sense I'm going to hear another piece of family history."

"Only if you want to. If it's boring you, I'll happily change the subject."

"I'm not bored. Just a little . . . overwhelmed."

Lamoral and Eurydike re-entered the ballroom. Crystal tinkled distantly from overhead. "Her name was Helen," Lamoral said, "and she started out as the daughter of the Duke of Bavaria. The next-to-last Habsburg, Franz-Josef, was supposed to marry her; but they didn't get on and poor old Franz-J. married her fifteen-year-old sister Sisi instead. So Helen married my ancestor Maximilian and built this place to outdo all of Vienna."

"I've seen Schönbrunn," said Eurydike. "She succeeded."

"Helen got her throne room, even if she wasn't entitled to sit down in it, and Sisi made Franz-Josef miserable all his days. Which doubtless pleased Helen also."

Eurydike gave him an appraising look. "Your family has a talent for revenge."

"We have a talent for survival," Lamoral corrected. "Survive long enough, and you're revenged on everybody."

"As witness the Habsburgs."

"I don't think they're witnessing much of anything these days." Lamoral looked at her. "Supper? You'll meet my sister. She actually runs the place."

"I'm starved."

He closed the door of the ballroom behind them, took Eurydike's arm, led her down the softly carpeted corridor. Gold leaf glowed softly from the walls. The countless clocks ticked away in their gilt and ivory cases.

"I've been wondering about your own family, actually," he said. "Is your hyphen the result of your marriage, or your ancestors'?"

She gave a chuckle. "Neither. It reflects an alliance between genetics and capital."

"I think the *Landadel* would understand that well enough."

"About twenty-five years ago the whole n-dimensional problem was beginning to be perceived, in embryo, as the next big thing in science. My legal guardian, Basil Apostolidis—"

"*That* Apostolidis?"

"The very same. His companies were into cutting-edge science and technology, and he knew that if he could beat the other technocrats to the punch, he could make a fortune— well, *another* fortune. So in typical freebooting Greek fashion he set out to build something that could solve the problem for him."

"Which was?"

"Me."

Lamoral stared at her, shocked. Eurydike burst out laughing. "Don't look at me like that!" she said. "I'm a damned successful experiment!"

"Just bred you? They didn't *ask*—"

"Who gets asked? Did they ask you if you wanted to be Inheritor-Prince? I'm a damn sight luckier than those four-armed killers whose chief occupation these days is waiting tables for the Party Set."

"You're right." He still felt a bit stunned. "I apologize."

"I suppose the idea must be a little startling to someone from another century. *Several* other centuries, I mean."

Waving her free arm at the schloss. "Anyway, most of my genetics came from a Japanese mathematician named Ichimonji, who had a Nobel and was considered top-of-the-mark, although a bit past his prime. A nice fellow, Ichiro, by the way, I met him lots of times before he died in the war. And I got some of Basil's genes, I guess because he couldn't resist, and some other genetics considered desirable for one reason or other. Some of Einstein's, some of—"

"Einstein? But he lived centuries ago. How did they—?"

"They've got lots of cells. His brain was preserved in a cardboard box behind a beer cooler in Kansas City." She saw his expression and laughed again. "To quote you quoting your friend quoting someone or other, you could look it up."

Lamoral blinked. "I don't believe I really want to know the truth behind that story, I'm afraid. It might turn out to be true."

"Basil created a full dozen of us, each with slightly different mixes of genetics, and we were each raised in a highly structured environment in which we were exposed to math and science."

"You were in Mexico City."

"Most of the time. Anyway, about half of us managed to resist the indoctrination and never turned out scientists. The rest got interested enough in science to start working on the problem. We'd do all our work separately and compare notes later. And I was the one who got the brass ring."

"And the Party Set?"

She shrugged. "Senility comes early to most mathematicians: we do our best work before we're thirty. I didn't want to spend my life trying to top my earlier work, so I took my millions in royalties and retired."

"After sitting out the war."

"I retired prior to the war. It was the Party Set that came after."

"Here's the dining room." He put his hand on the doorknob, then hesitated. "One question, if I may. How common is the kind of engineering that produced you?"

"It's not . . . unusual." She thought for a moment. "It's a labor-intensive and fairly elaborate procedure to create a human that way, so generally we're only built for special projects, but the war probably put the technology in a lot of hands that didn't have it before, so I'd say it's going to be increasingly commonplace from now on.''

The dining room was small by schloss standards: the 15th-century oak table, with its ebony-and-ivory inlaid frieze, seated only 16. There were only three place settings, all at one end, in order that the diners might avoid having to contemplate the ghastly mid-Victorian solid gold centerpiece, an unfortunate gift from the Wittelsbachs, who had made it out of metal "drizzled" out of the bullion epaulets and gold braid of their guardsmen.

Gloria rose from her seat, stepped forward across the parquet floor. Lamoral felt uneasy: she was frailer than she'd appeared on the comm unit. Lamoral took her hand, kissed her cheek.

"Gloria, may I present Eurydike Ichimonji-Apostolidis? My sister, Gloria Mariae.''

The two women clasped hands and murmured their hellos. Lamoral had been reserved the place at the head of the table, and signalled to the periwigged servant hovering near the door to bring the first wine and the first course.

Rather than reflect upon the Wittelsbach centerpiece he watched Eurydike and Gloria and wondered about all the careful genetic engineering that had gone into each. Gloria was the offspring of a 700-year breeding program, one carefully designed to conserve and extend a demonstrable talent for survival and the preservation and extension of wealth. The house of Thurn und Taxis wasn't a knightly house, with its fortune won by the sword; it had always been connected with capital, and never, unlike most of Europe's nobility, had to suffer the consequences of the chivalric code's disdain for working for a living. The 11th Prince had even gone so far as to chide the Prince Consort of England for his lack of industry. ("No workee," he said, "no money," and thereby ended forever his chances of hunting deer at Sandringham.) The family fortune was built on the transmission of data; it had never rejected the modern world.

Patience. Preservation. Adaptability. Survival above all. The watchwords of Gloria's ancestors; and if such things were carved in genetics, they were carved in Gloria's. Gloria did not, strictly speaking, live for herself: she lived for the family, for her elaborate web of ancestors and descendents.

Eurydike, on the other hand, had been created for a single task. There was something purposeful in her genetics, something singleminded and fierce, like a weapon created for a single deadly function—like, in fact, those four-armed warriors who, their war over, were good for little more than waiting tables. Now she had fulfilled her purpose, and fulfilled it very young. She had no more reason to exist.

Use it once and throw it away. The manufacturers' ethic had now been adapted to people.

Eurydike would have to adapt to a new life, and if she were successful, it would be because she discarded the ethic that had produced her and learned Thurn und Taxis virtues.

Lamoral raised his glass. "A toast, if I may."

The others looked at him expectantly.

"To breeding," he said.

Each woman smiled, no doubt for her own reasons.

The Dart dropped out of a cold Regensburg sky. "Thank you for your offer of hospitality," Eurydike said, "but I'm going to Bermuda and sleep until these little bits of war stop breaking out. During the last few years, people have just acquired the wrong habits. Maybe I'll rise for Edwardes' Christmas concert next year."

"I'll probably see you there." Lamoral turned up the collar of his overcoat.

The Dart made its silent landing on the rain-wet concrete pad. Eurydike turned to Lamoral and kissed him goodbye.

"See you next year."

"Bye."

Lamoral watched the Dart rise into the cloud cover, then returned to his auto and told it to take him back to the schloss. He had family to meet.

And plans to make. Party Set stock had suffered a double blow when Cao Cao's death was followed by the riot during the Day of the Dead.

The family, and the family bank, was buying.

Step One, Lamoral thought.

He didn't know what Step Two was yet, but was confident it would at some point evolve.

Christmas, 2145: for Lamoral, one Set-day later. While he was asleep, the Thurn und Taxis family had filed suit against the Party Set for damages suffered, during the war, on account of lack of guidance from the head of the family. The suit was settled out of court for an undisclosed sum. Though Lamoral wasn't fully cognizant of present currency values, it still seemed a whopping great sum.

So much for Step One. Waking up was getting to be a little more interesting.

Lamoral finished knotting his bow tie and turned to Alex.

"I don't know if I'd attend, were I you," he said, "considering what happened the last time you and Edwardes met."

"He was so far gone on Lilt he thought it was Cao Cao he was strangling."

"Don't be too sure. He knew me through my costume."

"It's that aura of noblesse that surrounds you, Lamoral. It's unmistakable."

Lamoral turned to the mirror again, buttoned his dinner jacket. "If I have it, you've got it."

"I'm the younger son, remember?"

"By twenty minutes."

"They're a very significant twenty minutes. They mark the difference between the anointed prince and the guy who gets to follow in his wake and play the practical jokes."

Lamoral looked at Alex. "No practical jokes tonight, Alex," he said.

"I've got a sack of rotten eggs for the tenor."

Lamoral hardened his look. "No, Alex."

Alex held his eyes for a moment, then turned away. "If you insist."

"Why would Edwardes want to strangle Cao Cao?"

Alex looked surprised. "Because of Lilt, of course."

"What about it?"

Alex gave a disbelieving grin. "You really don't understand about human weakness, do you?"

"Not Edwardes' weakness, anyway."

"Edwardes *needs* Lilt. Once his life was filled with his

career, but he gave that up. Helen Nomathemba was his first
substitute, but he lost *her*; and what's left is Lilt. And there
are no drawbacks with Lilt—no hangover, no loss of motor
coordination, no toxic effects at all. You have to saturate
yourself with it to get as soused as Edwardes gets. Practically
drown yourself in vats of it.''

''Yes.''

Alex was patient. ''You hate anything you need that badly,
don't you?''

Light dawned. ''Ah.'' Lamoral thought for a moment. ''If
he wants to destroy himself so much, why not use alcohol?''

Alex shrugged. ''Lilt doesn't wreck the voice.''

''Oh.''

Alex started for the door, put his hand on the knob. ''Perhaps it's only because he challenged me to a duel and then
tried to strangle me, but I suspect he's the chap that annihi-
lated Cao Cao.''

''I'm thinking the same thing.''

Alex stepped into the corridor. ''I wouldn't turn my back
on him.''

''I won't. Will you?''

They looked at each other for a moment, and then Alex
nodded.

''Understood,'' he said. ''I'll meet you on the Dart.''

''Indira isn't coming?'' Lamoral asked. Eurydike and Kitsune were off in a corner of the New Met's lobby, talking
with Carolly. Lamoral and Alex deposited with the cloak attendant two overcoats and two wraps, each covered with diamonds that the New York drizzle had strewn from the skies.
Lamoral noticed the attendant had an extra pair of arms.

Alex smiled and pocketed a pair of stubs. ''Indira *hates*
opera, Lamoral,'' he said. ''Some singers more than others.
I thought you knew.''

''And Kitsune doesn't?''

''Doesn't what? Hate opera, or know?''

''I'd just like to be kept abreast of who's trying to kill you
at any given moment.''

Alex's look was all innocence. ''No one's trying to kill
me, Lamoral. I've been telling you that.''

The lights blinked. "Time to find our box," Lamoral said.
Alex pirouetted. "Going to pat me down for rotten eggs?"
"I trust you."
A snicker. "That's a first."

Eurydike and Kitsune joined them and the four walked to
their box. Unger was in the next box with Darryl Wilson, the
actor, and a shared bottle, both commencing the destruction
of new livers. Mary Maude Mullen, having left Bermuda for
the first time in decades, was in the presidential box across
the hall. Lamoral was surprised she hadn't covered the box
in Union jacks and had the audience sing "God Save the
Queen" upon her entrance.

Kitsune and Alex chatted away till the lights began to dim,
but Eurydike seemed in a contemplative mood. Lamoral tried
several conversational sallies, but she failed to respond. Giving up, he opened his program and began to read.

"Stille Nacht," okay. "O Sole Mio," for all the people
who couldn't live without hearing it one more time. Spender's
"Stable Lass," a sentimental holiday favorite. Ending, before the interval, with the tenor aria from Messiah. After the
interval was Mozart's "Exsultate, Jubilate," which presumably had been written down from soprano to tenor, but which
should still contain enough high notes to keep Edwardes'
audience on the edge of their chairs. Otello again, a peculiar
choice in this context. Edwardes just couldn't stay away from
the part. Then an aria from Otake's Ran, the one where, after
the death of his loyal son, the Old Daimyo curses his remaining children. Lamoral could feel the hair on his neck
begin to lift. And after that was Judas's song from Night in
Jerusalem, wherein the betrayer makes up his mind to sell
Jesus to the Romans.

After which came "Deck the Halls," in which, Lamoral
understood from the program, the audience was supposed to
participate.

A Christmas concert, Lamoral thought. Right. Edwardes
was going to sing the most anguished, violent songs in his
repertoire, then try to cheer everyone up with a sing-along.
It would all be happy as a group sing at the court of King
Oedipus, Lamoral thought, with Jocasta keeping time,
swinging by the neck from the roofbeams.

The house lights dimmed. Lamoral watched Alex set his face into a condescending, slightly contemptuous mask. He couldn't throw eggs, but he could pretend Edwardes' voice wasn't up to the mark.

And again Alex was wrong. Rising like a flooding aural tide from the acoustic bowl of the New Met, Edwardes' voice was glorious, the best Lamoral had ever heard. Alex's display seemed petulant alongside such magnificence. No wonder Edwardes had put his voice on ice, revealed it only occasionally over the years—he would give another singer time to build a name and reputation, then make a carefully-crafted appearance like this and blow the newcomer out of the water. Edwardes was not aiming simply at immortality, but at deification: the new Apollo, God-King of the Tenors.

And he'd left the Lilt alone. There wasn't any happy smile, any false jolliness.

Alex was perhaps the only audience member—besides the Doyenne, of course—not on his feet at the end of the Handel. As the applause died down, Lamoral turned to Eurydike and smiled. "Excuse me, 1A," she said, and made her way out of the box.

Lamoral watched her go, smile frozen to his face, then left the box while the applause was still rising from the audience.

"I thought she should know," Carolly said, one short moment later. "Sorry if I upset you."

Carolly was on her way to the bar, flicking open and shut an antique Japanese lacquered fan ornamented with peacocks and ocean waves. Lamoral had given it to her decades ago.

"It's a little early to hand Eurydike this 1A stuff, don't you think?" Lamoral asked.

The fan opened, covered Carolly's face. One eye winked out, its green iris cold as a jade marble. "Better she should know now," muffled by the fan, "than find out as I did."

"You're being protective all of a sudden."

"She's new," Carolly said. "A bit vulnerable on that score."

"Eurydike's smarter than the two of us put together."

"I just told her the facts," she said. "It's more than you ever told me." The fan snapped closed, and with it the subject.

More pearls, Lamoral thought, for the recordings. He made an effort and unclenched his jaw. "Watch Edwardes tonight," he said.

An eyebrow lifted. "Isn't that what we're here for?"

"Watch the second act. Watch it with an eye towards . . . recent events."

"Ah."

"Tell me if I'm hallucinating."

Carolly smiled, a bit over-coldly. "You're hallucinating," she said.

Lamoral got a double cognac at the bar and drank it with slow, angry deliberation. He put down the empty snifter and started back to his box. Kitsune intercepted him.

"Cat's out of the bag, eh?"

"I would have told her. If things had progressed that far."

Kitsune put her arm through Lamoral's. "You're both rebounding from Sandy," she said. "Carolly wants a new protégée, and is going to be more protective of this one than of the last, and you . . . well, your interest is a little more obvious."

"Thanks so much," said Lamoral.

Kitsune tossed her long hair. "Give it time. She's new."

Eurydike was back in the box, feigning genteel interest in her program, when Lamoral and Kitsune arrived. Alex gave Lamoral a sympathetic look. Lamoral seated himself and leaned toward Eurydike.

"I would have told you," Lamoral said.

Her look was cooler than he would have liked. "I'm not upset."

"I hope to hell not."

She offered him a slight smile. Lights dimmed, and it was time for Mozart.

Edwardes' second half was staggering. Never had Lamoral seen so much emotional power concentrated on a stage. Without props or costumes, Edwardes called up the 16th century, first a man tearing away at the rags of civilization that covered his anguished, raving, violent soul; and then, switching from Italian to Japanese, Edwardes created a man brought to nothing, no hope, no future, no family, nothing but impotent rage and desolation, waving fists and spouting curses at an indifferent sky. His massive form seemed to shrink; under a cool blue spotlight he seemed a scrawny old man, half-starved, dressed in silken rags. His Judas, after all this, was surprisingly tranquil, a man resolving formally to perform an act he'd long ago made up his mind to do, a deed that somehow put his mind at peace—and that interpretation, somehow, seemed more unsettling than anything that had preceded it.

"Deck the Halls" came as a considerable relief, to Lamoral as well as the rest of the audience. Lamoral mopped his brow and left the box while the audience was singing the first chorus. He needed to make a phone call.

He got Helmsley out of bed, but the detective's robot eyes were unclouded by sleep.

"I know who killed Cao Cao," Lamoral said. "It was Thomas Edwardes."

"Can you prove it?"

"Look at the vid of the Christmas concert. I've never seen anything more revealing in my life. It was a virtual confession."

Helmsley was silent for a long moment. Then, "I don't think so."

"Look at the vid!"

"I will. But I don't think Edwardes did it."

Lamoral stared at the phone screen. "How can you say that?" he said finally.

"Edwardes is a passionate man. A performer. He acts out every emotion as it comes to him, and his emotions are very close to the surface. If he'd chilled Cao Cao, I would almost certainly have detected it in the initial interrogation. He's so open that I very much doubt he could have hidden it from me."

Lamoral shook his head. "Look at the concert, superintendent."

"I will."

"He's an actor, remember, not just a singer. During the interrogation he could have been acting the part of an innocent man, and done it with conviction."

Lamoral detected a hint of skepticism breaking through Helmsley's deadpan. "I'll look at the vid, but I make no promises. The file was closed months ago, and I'll need more evidence than a concert recording to get it reopened.''

Lamoral blanked the screen without saying goodbye. He went to the bar, had another double cognac, and waited for Edwardes to finish his encores. After a while Lamoral got tired of waiting and went back to the box.

The crowd was baying its pleasure. Even Alex was on his feet applauding, though his expression showed he was just being polite. Edwardes did his fourth encore—the *"Exsultate"* again—then waved and skipped off the stage.

"He'll be Lilted to the ears by midnight," Kitsune predicted.

The reception afterward had only a few hundred people, mostly Party Set and New York's government. The mayor handed Edwardes a key to the city; Edwardes gave a Lilting grin and raised the key in one big hand.

"You're upset," Lamoral said later. It was their first moment away from the others.

Eurydike looked at him. "I told you I wasn't."

"I didn't know that you didn't know. If you'd been watching Set recordings . . .''

"I was solving the mysteries of the universe. Sorry."

Lamoral tried to make a joke. "We could make it morganatic," he smiled. "If it came to that."

Her face was stony. "How many 1As are there, anyway?"

"Thousands, I suppose. Before I joined the Set I used to get introductions all the time." He made a face. "Suitable women."

"I can't believe that this kind of medieval thing still goes on. Don't peers marry showgirls all the time?"

"English peers can, I guess. But if one of the *Landadel* did, the *Almanach de Gotha* would degrade the whole pedigree to—''

Her eyebrows arched. "1B?"

"Second, at least. Or third." Laughing, still trying to make a joke out of it.

She shuddered in mock horror. "And then the sky would *really* fall."

He looked at her. "I didn't invent this, you know."

"So you can't breed an heir with me. Or if you did, the rules would disinherit him right at the start."

"There are ways around everything, Eurydike."

"I can just imagine."

Lamoral thought for a moment, trying to find a way to explain things. "One doesn't live entirely for oneself, you know. There are responsibilities that extend from generation to generation."

"Right. Keeping the castles up, avoiding inheritance taxes, keeping the clocks wound . . ." She gave a snarl. "Snobbery! My God, as if any of it mattered!"

"The Set isn't based on snobbery?"

"*I'm* not, whatever the Set is."

"You're new to the Set, Eurydike. The first thing you learn is that there is plenty of time for everything. I didn't think you'd want to drop out of the Set, get married, and start producing children quite so soon."

Eurydike linked her arm with his, looked up at him. "I'm not as upset as you seem to think I am, Lamoral. This whole pedigree thing is just," searching for the word, "*emblematic* of something else. That I *am* young, that I *am* new to the Set."

"Yes."

"That I've lived in one Apostolidis fortress or another all my life, and that I need a few flights of freedom before I deal with yet another set of formidable ancestors. Castles, servants in wigs, thrones that one can or can't sit on, all that."

He might as well, Lamoral thought, surrender with grace. " '*Wenn ihr einer dem andern euch an den Mund hebt und ansetzt—: Getränk an Getränk: o wie entgeht dann der Trinkende seltsam der Handlung.*' "

" 'When you lift yourselves to each other's lips,' " she said, raising herself to him; her lips were moist. " 'Drink unto drink.' " Again and again. " 'O how strangely the drinker eludes . . . *her* . . . part.' " Correcting for gender.

She turned, to find a VTO to take her back to Bermuda and frozen time. Lamoral watched her collect her wrap and go out into the sleet; and afterwards he saw Edwardes' key in the trash.

* * *

Another Set-day; another phone call.

"Good afternoon, Gloria."

"Hello, Lamoral. Where are you now?"

"In Lhasa. Buddha's about to walk down from Heaven, and then we're going to have a party."

Gloria gave a cold smile. "Good for him, dear, to take a look around every now and again."

"One gathers he does it every year."

Gloria's smile thinned. "Have you ever considered the parallels between the Buddha and yourself?"

Buddhalike, Lamoral gave it his consideration. "I'm afraid it never occurred to me."

"Are you enjoying the mountains?"

Lamoral had to think about that one. He shifted in his seat. "They make me uneasy, truth to tell. I have to keep telling myself that I don't *do* that anymore."

"I don't see why not. It would look lovely on television—you could make a Set event of it."

"It wouldn't be the same. And Alex never liked it as well as I did."

Gloria gave a lift to her shoulders, one too subtle to be called a shrug. "You didn't have to bring him along in the first place. I never understood why you did, if he wasn't keen on it."

"He didn't complain."

Gloria barked out a laugh. Light danced in her flinty eyes. "Where would complaint have got him?"

"It probably wouldn't have got him up any mountains, anyway."

"I suppose not." She looked at him carefully. "I haven't seen him in years, you know. I wish you'd apply your famous strong arm and coerce him into paying a visit."

"I thought I had. I'll have to be stronger, I suppose."

"Thank you. Every time I see him, it's a recording, and he's doing something inappropriate. It makes me want to shake him."

"I'm familiar with the urge."

She looked up, eyes alert. "You could come yourself, you know. It's hunting season. You could shoot a boar or two."

Lamoral smiled. "I haven't done that in . . . how long?"

"The last big boar hunt—the last you attended, anyway—was after you graduated from university."

"It was never my favorite sport. A little static for my taste."

"Yes, but the boars do need clearing out every so often. Otherwise they start digging up the gardens and raiding rubbish dumps."

"Yes, I'll come by and shoot a few."

"I wish you would."

"And I'll put the arm on Alex."

"Very good."

Lamoral thought about the last boar hunt, the year after graduation, with the beaters in their tabards and huntsmen in green leather, the echoing roar of the heavy rifles, the pleasant toot of horns, the scent of coffee poured from the antique vacuum bottles with their silver fittings . . .

He smiled.

Plan Two had just occurred to him.

Sunset flamed along the gold-and-vermilion walls of the Potala. Lamoral looked out at the mountains beyond and felt a taste of longing touch his tongue.

He didn't *do* that anymore, he reminded himself.

"I'd stay clear of Edwardes if I were you, Lamoral." Unger's voice was heavy in his ear. "A microcamera recorded that phone call of yours last year, the one to Bermuda."

"Ah," Lamoral said. A faint alarm chimed in his mind. "Now he'll want to strangle me *and* my brother."

"He's angry enough to do it." Unger gave a laugh. "An interesting picture, don't you think, one of you dangling in either of Edwardes' hands?"

Lamoral looked at him. Even though Unger was carrying a cocktail shaker and a couple of glasses, he didn't seem as drunk as usual. But then, of course, the night was young.

"We'll all have to be a lot more careful," Unger said. "Recorders were damn near microscopic before, but now thanks to Eurydike they can hide the things in the nth dimension."

"Have you told Alex?" Lamoral asked.

"About Edwardes? What difference would it make?"

Lamoral considered. "None, I suppose. You're right there."

"You have a respite. He's not in Lhasa, he's resting on his frozen laurels back in Bermuda."

"Good."

"Tell you what," Unger said. "I'll write a poem about bloodshed, and you can accuse me next. It'll boost my royalties."

"Only if I get a cut, Unger."

Tonight the Party was being held in a domed restaurant and nightclub, built in the shape of a steel-and-crystal lotus 400 meters high. There were hints that His Omniscience the Dalai Lama might choose to drop by later and pay his respects, one immortal to another.

Cymbals clattered on the bandstand as the drummer, setting up, dropped his equipment. Lamoral turned at the sound. The Party Set was finishing predinner cocktails and sitting down at tables along with an assortment of robed monks and Tibetan and Chinese officials. Lamoral could see Alex with Indira Batish, Eurydike sharing a table with Carolly, Kitsune chatting to one of the musicians.

"Buy you a drink?" Unger asked. He raised a cocktail shaker in one hand and a pair of glasses in the other.

Lamoral shrugged. "Why not?"

They both looked up as something flashed up above. Through the clear dome they could see a bright rift appearing in the violet Tibetan sky, a widening slit through which golden light poured . . .

"Is this on the program?" Unger wondered. Lamoral shaded his eyes.

Suddenly there was a wide stairway extending from the bright hole in the sky, gilded and ruddy like the vermilion face of the Potala. The stair descended in a rainbow arc toward Lhasa, but like a rainbow faded to nothingness as it approached the ground.

Lamoral's heart leaped into his throat. A figure was moving on the stair, descending from out of the golden light toward the ground. The figure was hundreds of meters tall. He was dressed in an elaborate brocaded robe and a tall gold headdress on which the heads of gods and demons were carved—except that the heads all seemed to be alive, their mouths speaking something no one could hear, their eyes rolling in unison.

Chaos burst out in the dining room, people shouting, rushing for a better view. Monks began to chant sutras.

Lamoral watched as the figure slowly descended the stairs, then vanished into the darkness of the Lhasa valley. The rift in the sky sealed up.

"Good trick," said Unger. He poured from the shaker into his two glasses.

Lamoral turned and looked at Eurydike. She was still staring, openmouthed, at the darkened sky.

"I think this was one of Eurydike's," Lamoral said.

"God from the nth dimension," Unger said. "Is that in her equations?"

"It is now."

Unger drained a glass. "Just think what we're going to get come Christmas." He drained the other. "Oh dear," he said conversationally. "I seem to have carelessly consumed your drink as well as mine."

"Go right ahead," Lamoral said. "I have a feeling the rest of the evening's going to be anticlimactic anyway."

Lamoral was right about that: the Dalai Lama never showed up, no doubt trying to rationalize the unexpected event from his own perspective, and Eurydike spent the night at a corner table with a portable computer and several pads of paper, trying to work out how the trick had been done. Lamoral got into his Hirondel and left early, rising into the moonlit sky. No rifts appeared; no giant figures stalked across the night.

An impulse took him.

"Computer," Lamoral said. "Change the destination, please. Take me to the summit of K2."

The computer thought about that one. "There is no landing field at that location," it said, "and strong winds may make a landing inadvisable."

"Do it anyway," Lamoral said.

Wind buffeted the Hirondel as it came to a landing, but the computer was up to the job. Lamoral put on his anorak and zipped the collar up past his chin.

"Open the door, computer," he said.

"That would be inadvisable," the computer said. "The oxygen content of the air is such that prolonged exposure may result in brain damage."

"I won't be outside long enough for brain damage to occur."

"My program will not allow me to open the door."

Lamoral sighed inwardly. "Emergency override. This is Lamoral, Fürst von Thurn und Taxis."

There was a moment while the computer voiceprinted him, then the door reluctantly slid open.

Even before he left the VTO the cold wind cut through his clothes like a blade. Lamoral stepped out onto bare rock and saw the sprawl of the Himalayas below him. Rock folded into shadow; opalescent snow gleamed in the moonlight. The mountain's plume streamed out below his feet.

It had been over 50 years since he'd last enjoyed this view.

He circled the Hirondel, getting it all. He remembered the bright sunlight on his first ascent, the way the little cell-powered engine whined near his ear, refining oxygen out of the air, feeding it into his mask. He remembered Karl-August Hormayr's bright orange parka, the Austrian flag gleaming red-and-white on his shoulder. Alex capering like a madman at the summit, his howls torn away by the furious blast. The darkness of the noontime sky. Bright spiralling powder carried in silver curtains by the dancing wind . . .

His lungs pumped like bellows in the faint air. His extremities had already gone numb. If he didn't get in the VTO right away he was going to lose something to frostbite.

Besides, he didn't do this anymore.

He got in the Hirondel and told it to take him to Regensburg.

He was going to shoot a couple of boar and think about Plan Two.

The next Set-day, Eurydike was awarded the Nobel Prize, and everyone went to Stockholm for the party. A Set-day later, Alex and Indira had a screaming argument in the lounge of the floating Palace of Kanayasha, but the Set-day following they made it up at a party staged in high-Earth orbit. During the subsequent Adjustment, a terribly dull Malagasque Professor delivered a lecture about *n*-dimensional pocket universes, the Buddha's appearance being a "reverse dimensional manifestation," and even Eurydike had trouble following it.

A fraction of a Set-day later, Lamoral and Alex were awakened by a call from Regensburg—it was part of the agreement that settled their suit with the Party Set that Regensburg could so awaken them—and, while the Lilt still buzzed in their brains, courteous and sympathetic Adjustors told them that Gloria had died in her sleep.

The funeral and other arrangements took a week of realtime. Gloria's second child, Claudius, was put in charge of the family business, the first child having taken her trust fund and fired herself in the general direction of the constellation Hercules, from which red-shifted correspondence arrived at dutiful intervals.

Claudius was informed of Plans One and Two. He approved of both.

The next Set-day was a Party Barge trip to the Sea of Moscow on the far side of Luna. "I've seen Moscow," Alex said, blinking out of the dome at the grey desolation, "and I've seen its Sea, and neither can be said to improve the other." Though it had been objective months since Gloria's death, Lamoral still felt the loss slicing into his throat like a sharp mortal blade. Carolly hovered around him and thankfully prevented him from harming himself or others.

During the next Adjustment the Party Set were informed of the case of Diane Demetrios, who had been refused Set membership, on account of cosmetic surgery, 'way back in the previous century, and who, in her wealthy old age, had used genetic technology to create three perfect Setwomen, intending a triumph in the second generation. All three had been likewise refused, and had then been snuffed by their irate creator, who had in turn been sentenced to spend the rest of her existence in something called a "punitive pocket universe."

"Hell, I presume," said Alex cheerfully.

The Set considered it terrific publicity. Though stock fell at first report, it subsequently rose in heavy trading. Ratings and membership applications went up.

Claudius informed Lamoral that during the brief stock fall, the family bank had bought heavily, and though a considerable paper profit had been made, the family and its associates were approaching their limit. If the takeover plan were to continue, outsiders would have to be brought in.

Plan Two was plotted in detail.

Gloria's death kept digging talons into Lamoral's heart.

Next Set-day, Lamoral presented his plan for a full-scale Regensburg boar-hunt to the Party Set's Board of Directors. Mary Maude Mullen seized the idea with her every fang, though because Set events were planned so far in advance quite a number of sidereal years would have to elapse before the thing could be slotted into the schedule.

Lamoral smiled and said thank-you.

Later in the day, as the Party bobbed along in a glass-walled nautilus at the bottom of the Marianas Trench, Lamoral saw Eurydike dance the tango with a man named Mohammed Abu Minyar al-Mulazim, who was not yet a member of the Set but was understood to be a likely candidate . . . and though Lamoral very much wanted to do something Alex-like and conspicuous, he decided to keep Carolly's company instead.

As Edwardes, in the next chamber of the curled nautiloid shell, was moved spontaneously to burst into the Old Daimyo's aria again, Lamoral listened to the sound vibrating through the structure of the ship and wondered if Carolly had planned all this somehow.

He never found out one way or another.

Ten Set-days later, three years realtime, the Party Set was shuffled to Regensburg to sign the Visitors' Book. Lamoral stood by the door and watched one long, low car after another drive up, breathe out beautiful people, then draw them back in.

"You won't have to," Lamoral told Eurydike, as she stepped onto the curb. "You've already signed."

She looked at him, then thought for a moment. Remembrance crossed her face. "Aha!" she said. "You had me sign the book, then step outside, then come in again."

"No one gets inside on the first visit," Lamoral said.

She gave him a slight frown. "Another one of those traditions you daren't meddle with, Lamoral?"

At least, Lamoral reflected, she hadn't called him 1A.

"This particular tradition has its uses," he said. "It kept Hitler out."

Eurydike thought about that one.

The custom applied only to commoners, but Lamoral decided it would be impolitic to point that out, especially to Eurydike. If Hitler had been an aristocrat, then-Prince Albert would have had to swallow his distaste and receive him.

"Hitler had his revenge, of course," Lamoral continued. "He held the Inheritor-Prince hostage during the latter part of the war, and requisitioned one of our castles for use as a decoy target for bombers."

"Leaving you with how many others?"

"Twenty-two. But only if you only count actual castles. We've actually got forty-odd chateaux in Europe."

She nodded. "Of course."

"I can't help it, you know, if I own castles." Lamoral nodded at Darryl Wilson as the actor eased himself out of his limousine. "Just as you can't help the fact you were born to do prize-winning mathematics."

"I'd like to think that I rose above the circumstances of my birth."

"Lucky lady," Lamoral said, shaking hands with Wilson.

Eurydike arched an eyebrow. "Does that indicate a degree of envy, Lamoral?"

Wilson walked into the entry hall to put his shaky signature in the book. "You were designed to be used and thrown away," Lamoral said. "Anyone who can rise above that deserves, if not precisely my envy, at least my admiration."

There was a moment's resentful silence. "*Is* there anyone you envy, Lamoral?"

Lamoral processed this question with care. "Another person might possess abilities that I wish were mine," he said finally. "But do I wish I were that person? No." He held her eyes. "Truthfully, no."

"That sort of self-possession is rare. Even among the Set."

"The Set is too obsessed with examining itself to be truly

at ease. Probably the result of all those cameras being poked at us all the time.''

''I suppose so.'' She gnawed her lip. ''How safe is this boar hunt going to be, Lamoral? You're going to be arming all these people with great heavy rifles, and one of them may be—*is*—a killer.''

''Every Set event is recorded, remember? Whoever killed Cao Cao did it in such a way that he or she wouldn't be discovered. Would such a careful assassin give himself away by shooting at a fellow Setman in front of an audience of millions?''

''I don't know. Would he?''

''I think not.''

Her expression was stolid. ''I hope you're right.''

''Most of them will be lucky to hit a boar.'' He smiled lightly. Eurydike's look didn't change.

Another car rolled up: Mohammed al-Mulazim stepped out, gave Lamoral and Eurydike a friendly wave. He'd officially passed the Doyenne's inspection two Set-days ago.

''I think I'll move on, Lamoral,'' she said.

Lamoral watched as she pecked Mohammed's cheek, then walked past Mohammad and left in his limo. Lamoral held out his hand and smiled in welcome; Mohammed took it.

A Set-month slid by, spent whirlwind-fashion in 20-odd fortresses of pleasure, the new resort in orbit around Sol, another on the Great Barrier Reef, a Christmas at La Scala for another of Edwardes' comebacks: and then the long cars, black and grey, carried the Party Set from the nearest Regensburg landing field to Schloss St. Emmeram once more. For once they would employ beds for the purposes of sleep; in the morning they would hunt boar.

The new eavesdropping technology had, Lamoral was informed, been conquered. A small device could be purchased that would spot any camera popping out of the nth dimension and zap it with an electron beam before it could do anything other than take a single still photo. The zappers were deployed in force: whole squadrons of illegal bugs were shot down in flames. The only pictures getting out of Regensburg would be Set-authorized ones.

Authorized recorders hovering in the background, the marble-columned banquet hall was put to use, one large enough to contain any number of Everlasting Diets. Lamoral sat at one end, with Carolly and Claudius flanking him; Alex was at the other, next to Indira. The brothers were wearing ribbons and decorations, the sort one got more or less automatically for being what they were—it would have been ridiculous to wear them to other functions, but in these surroundings they were not out of place. Mary Maude Mullen sat in the middle, directly opposite the hideous Wittelsbach centerpiece, which had been moved from the smaller dining room just for her enjoyment.

Lamoral was surprised at how Claudius had aged; he had become an old man, with powdery hair and broken veins in his cheeks. But he was a good businessman for all that, and had put together a very discreet investment combine that was prepared to make a takeover bid on the Party Set the very second the successful boar hunt was broadcast to the world's millions.

The first course appeared. The servants were wearing their more formal costumes for this appearance, including powdered wigs; Lamoral tried not to notice the incongruity of the 18th-century dress as measured against the occasional extra pair of arms, or in one case whiplike tentacles.

Carrying a tray stacked high with plates, one servant rolled past on what looked like giant ball bearings. "For the first time," Lamoral said, "I'm beginning to feel a little out of touch with things."

"The feeling will pass," Carolly said. She was examining Greek goddesses on the Cellini salt cellar. "It always does." She gave a look down the length of the table. "Have you noticed that Edwardes is drinking wine tonight?"

Lamoral looked down the table. "Not Lilt?" Edwardes was holding out a gold-rimmed goblet—a large one meant for mineral water, not wine—to one of the wine stewards.

"The last set of reviews," Carolly said, "the ones for La Scala, were not kind."

Lamoral had not attended; he made a policy of forbidding himself certain associations.

"He had too much Lilt in him," Carolly continued. "The

voice was good, but his control was gone. Among other things, he giggled too much."

"So now he's taken up a more destructive addiction."

"If the next concert's a failure, he can blame his choice of intoxicants."

Lamoral sipped his smoky Geisenheim and realized with a pang that the wine had been laid down by Gloria decades ago. "Perhaps I should have a word with the wine steward," he said.

"Do not interfere with people's methods of going to Hell, Lamoral," Carolly said, "and they won't interfere with yours."

Lamoral looked at her, a revelation rolling through his heart. He had heard that tone from her many times before and never, never had he realized what it meant.

"Is that why you're here, Carolly?" he asked. "To watch people send themselves to Hell?"

"It passes the time," Carolly said. Her eyes were cold green stone.

Lamoral looked at the assembled company and wondered why he'd let them into his home. This had always been the place he could retreat to, when the Set grew too onerous: now they were here, an occupying army, and Schloss St. Emmeram would not be the same even after they'd gone.

Eurydike located Lamoral in his office, in the old abbey, where the rooms were little and crooked and worn, furnished largely with stuff taken from Schloss Taxis in the 19th century, furnishings that didn't quite fit the small proportions of the old abbey and had either been left there, a bit out of scale, or hacked to fit. The old wing seemed vaguely Dickensian, quaint and odd and somehow comforting, without the lavish proportions of the rest of the palace. Pictures of people, all dead, hung on the walls.

"I was hoping," she said, "to get a dance out of you tonight."

Eurydike wore effortlessly a black strapless dress shot with silver threads; there was black jasper at her earlobes and throat. She kicked one foot back and cocked her body as if for a dance, her arms holding an invisible partner.

Lamoral, in his shirtsleeves and ribbon, took his feet off his desk and leaned his creaking old chair toward her. "A cognac first?"

She accepted and perched on his desk. "Aren't you supposed to be playing the host?"

"I felt the need for a moment of meditation."

"And I interrupted. Sorry."

"The moment passed." He sipped cognac. Fire made a welcome progress through his sinuses. His eyes strayed to a picture of Gloria. "I was thinking how much I miss my sister."

"I only met her that once, but I liked her."

Lamoral said nothing.

"We Set people," Eurydike said, "we have all our tragedies concentrated in such a short time, don't we? Parents die, then siblings die, and it all seems very fast to us. We barely have a chance to get over one death, and then there's another. And everyone's being gay around us, always."

"Let's not forget the wars." Thinking of Sandy, whose picture was not present, and which, he realized, needed to be.

"War. Let's hope there's only the one." She raised her glass and drank a silent toast to that notion. Lamoral followed her example.

"This was Hornmayer, yes? The climber who died?" Inspecting a picture on his desk.

"Hormayr. Karl-August."

"He died, and you joined the Set and never climbed another mountain. I thought that was very romantic when I was young."

Lamoral looked at her. "I thought you told me you spent your youth in a mathematical frenzy and never watched Set recordings."

She gave a throaty laugh. "I wasn't entirely immune to popular culture. I had quite a crush on you, actually, when I was a girl."

"Good God." Lamoral blinked. He had never thought of himself as schoolgirl crush material.

"Somehow I never found out about the 1A business, though."

"As I told you." Frowning. "There are ways around everything."

"Like inheritance taxes."

"Yes." He regarded her. "The climbing wasn't very romantic. It was just something I did. Then something I stopped doing."

"And when Hornmayer—Hormayr—died, that didn't have anything to do with it?"

"Certainly it did. But it didn't have *everything* to do with it." Eurydike seemed skeptical. Lamoral sipped cognac. "When you grow up like I did, in a place like this, you want to know what you're really capable of. You want to do something that you can accomplish not because of money or training, but something that you can do for yourself. Because you want to know what you're made of, exclusive of the titles and chateaux and all that. In olden times, someone like me would just put on a suit of armor and go off to a crusade or something. But that isn't desirable anymore, thank God, so I went up mountains instead."

"And you found out what you were made of."

"I did. And once I did, then I didn't have to do it anymore."

She leaned toward him and gave a slight frown. "I sense a certain elision here, but I won't press it."

Mutely elided by all the most exquisite joys . . .

"Thank you." He stood. "I should get back to my guests."

She reached out, touched the watered silk ribbon. "What is this, exactly?"

He shrugged on his jacket. "Order of the Golden Fleece."

"And what did you do to get it?" Taking his arm.

"I'll be damned if I remember."

They laughed.

"I probably gave a lot to charity," Lamoral considered. "That's usually what you get these for nowadays. Good works."

"Better than beating people over the head with swords."

"Indeed yes." He raised his snifter. "To plowshares."

The crystal rang; they both drank deep. Linking arms, they headed for the ballroom.

"You seem," he ventured, "not to be with Mohammed these days."

"He joined the Set, you see," thoughtfully. "And I found he became a lot less interesting once I realized I'd have to spend eternity with him."

"I sympathize."

"And you and Carolly?"

"Finished." Recalling her look at dinner.

"That was sudden."

"It's happened before. Less suddenly, but then we ought to be used to it."

"I sense another elision here." She took a breath. "Don't step on me when we dance tonight, Lamoral. You might be wrecking something."

"I'll take particular care."

And he did; the dance was very nice. He kissed her at the end of it, and then had to break up a brawl between Edwardes and Unger, who seemed to have uncovered a fundamental personality clash now that they were both soused on the same intoxicant. "I want to talk to you!" Edwardes said, as Lamoral hauled him away. Lamoral took his hands off the man, straightened his jacket, turned. "If you don't listen," Edwardes said darkly, "you're going to be sorry."

"To hell with you," Lamoral said.

"I'll be waiting outside," Edwardes said.

The ball went on, couples rotating in infinite profusion in the mirrors of the white spun-sugar ballroom, a diamond-perfect setting for the self-absorbed Set. Lamoral circulated, playing host. By and by the orchestra fell silent; the recorders were turned off, and people began drifting toward bed. Unger sat on the trestle-table, keeping the punch bowl company. Musicians packed their instruments. Carolly and Eurydike drifted about the cavernous white room, both waiting for Lamoral, somehow knowing better than to talk to each other.

Lamoral thanked the orchestra conductor for her efforts and shook, after a moment of hesitation, her lower right hand. He saw, over the conductor's shoulder, Indira Batish steaming out of the throne room, daggers shooting rapidfire from her eyes, and knew there was a crisis somewhere.

He crossed to the throne room door and opened it. A complex tangle of long, pale limbs were visible on the red-and-gold throne; it took some effort to sort them out into Alex and Kitsune. Kitsune was wearing the ribbon of Alex's Order of St. Maurice and St. Lazarus and not much else. Alex had Kitsune's diamond tiara hanging off one ear.

Lamoral carefully closed the door.

Did he hear Alex's laugh right then? Perhaps he did.

He saw Carolly speaking to one of the musicians, Eurydike talking to Unger. It occurred to him that it would be the height of gaucherie to treat Carolly as Alex had just treated Indira.

He winced. This was going to be a trying evening.

He'd have to tell Eurydike he'd be longer than he'd thought.

When, his face burning from Carolly's slap, he finally left the ballroom, he saw Edwardes sprawled on the marble floor just outside the door, where he'd fallen asleep waiting to give Lamoral the benefit of his wisdom.

"The Hung Breakfast," Carolly said on entering, loud enough for everyone to hear. Unger and Darryl Wilson, both battling hangover, winced. Kitsune, sharing Alex's corner of the table, laughed and offered brief applause.

It was before dawn; many of the Set had probably not slept at all. Lamoral and Eurydike certainly hadn't.

Lamoral had given careful orders about the amount of intoxicants permitted before the hunt. Just enough to take the edge off the hangovers, not enough to encourage carelessness with firearms.

Even so, he'd made sure that Unger and Edwardes were on the opposite end of the line from Alex and himself. If Edwardes decided to finally fight his duel with Alex, he'd have to thrash his way across half a league of underbrush before he ran into the spot of woods where Alex was placed. And the recorders would see everything.

But Edwardes hadn't appeared for breakfast. A footman told Lamoral he hadn't left his room.

Silverware clattered as the Hunt Breakfast was consumed. People in livery—in this informal setting, Lamoral had spared them the wigs—poured from silver Redfern coffee pots. Eurydike shrugged her right shoulder uncomfortably, trying to adjust the padding in her jacket—they would be using 19th- and 20th-century weapons that didn't spare the recoil.

"I hope I don't break anything," she said.

"There's always a risk," Lamoral said. His jaw still ached where Carolly had hit him.

"That gun's so bloody heavy."

"Sorry. But they don't make modern weaponry for boar. And it would look bad—radar-homing smart bullets are hardly a sportsman's weapon."

"One of those four-armed guys could probably take one on hand-to-hand."

"Possibly, but my money's on the boar."

"Did you hear? The ex-mayor of Guadalajara committed suicide."

"Couldn't have happened to a nicer person." He thought about the Set's four-armed bouncers. "D'you suppose the Set had anything to do with it?"

"Everything, but not the way you mean. It's a media age, and one takes a chance insulting a media icon like the Set. He never got good coverage again, no matter what he did, and that finished his political career."

People finished their coffees. Lamoral stood up and announced it was time for the hunters to head for the hills.

"Good," Carolly said, rising and flinging back her cape with a gesture that made Lamoral's jaw ache all over again. "I'm in the mood to kill something."

Lamoral put on his hat and cape, then took his rifle from the rack on the wall and broke it open over one arm. It was a double-barreled top-break single-shot by Heym, dated 1892, with an elephant-ivory stock chased, by Fabergé, with silver. It was a lovely gun: modern plastic weapons simply didn't have the elegance, let alone the perfect balance, of the fine old weapons.

Outside, the cheerful, chattering beaters were loading into vans. Mostly students, they were equipped with wicked boar-spears, the type with the T just below the point so the boar couldn't run himself up the length of the spear and mangle the huntsman. They also wore bright red-and-blue tabards, which added to the medieval flair of the proceedings but which were principally designed to make certain no one mistook them for a boar—and even if someone did, the tabards were bulletproof. Standing around the court-yard, gamekeepers in green tufted caps and green loden capes tooted their horns experimentally.

The hunters gathered round—out of all the Party Set, there were only 19 competent to bear arms, and the rest would cheer them on from the comfort of Schloss St. Emmeram. One of the gamekeepers carefully explained the rules of the hunt—they were elaborate, to assure none of the beaters or hunters getting shot—and then the keepers loaded into their cars and headed for the forest. The long limousines began to roll up, and Lamoral's guests headed for the game park.

Edwardes hadn't shown up.

During the drive to the forest dawn made an honest effort to appear, but largely failed. December frost limned the trees; the dark trunks were swathed in mist. Lamoral's breath paled out in front of him as he stood on the far right of the extended line of hunters and waited for the signal to begin. The scene was romantic and Teutonic as all hell: if he'd custom-ordered a day like this it couldn't be any better. The only anachro-nism, besides Darryl Wilson's white Stetson, was the silver-skinned Party Set VTO that settled onto the paved road be-hind them. It contained the two techs who controlled the recording equipment and the bug-zappers, which had cleared the woods of cameras and microphones.

A brisk horn signal echoed off the trees, was caught by the other horns and repeated. Lamoral felt his blood surge. Time to begin. Lamoral dropped a .470 Nitro Express slug into each barrel and snapped the breech shut, hearing the solid clunk of the Anson & Deeley action as it cocked the internal hammers. He made certain the safety was on. Some of the hunters made yipping noises as they stepped out from the starting line. Stupid, Lamoral thought, it would scare off the pigs.

Lamoral threw his cape back over his right shoulder and kept his eyes to the front. Mist and snow covered the ground in patches. The boar liked thick country and the underbrush was heavy. It would be all too easy to trip and fall; carrying a gun, that would be a bad idea. The beaters made distant whistling and rapping noises. Lamoral's careful footfalls released the scent of pine needles.

A booming shot: Lamoral's nerves leaped. Another, and another. Misses, Lamoral thought, all of them. Then there was another, deeper boom, and silence. The boar had been driven in front of another hunter, who had finished it.

Lamoral raised one foot to step over a fallen branch, then heard something rustle in front of him. He remained that way, one foot high, for a long second, then slowly lowered the foot to its original position and slid the safety off. He put the gun to the padded leather shoulder of his jacket and felt the coolness of the ivory cheekpiece against his face. Only when he was certain of his balance did he put his forefinger inside the trigger guard.

His senses strained into the mist. Something was rattling dead twigs out there, but it could be anything: a deer, someone's dog, a poacher caught in the middle of the landlord's hunt.

A bristling black shape raced out on short legs, saw him, spun on its hind trotters. Lamoral saw a flash of red eyes, of white ivory. His shot, all pure instinct, sent a ton of half-frozen snow cascading into his hat from the tree overhead. He held his stance for a short moment while his senses caught up: snow, shot, numbed shoulder, dead pig. The slug had exploded the tusker's heart like a brick dropped on a snowball.

He removed his finger from the trigger guard, broke the gun, discarded the smoking cartridge, and stepped over the fallen branch. His heart gave a yip of triumph. The pig was an old male, its tusks chipped and yellow, and after the hunt was over the gamekeepers would blow a special horn salute to the monster, and send it on its way to Valhalla with a piece of fir between its teeth. Then a bit of pine branch would be dabbled in the creature's blood, and the pine placed in Lamoral's hatband—ceremonies that went back far beyond his family's appearance in Bavaria, back to the time when the Teutons worshipped Wotan and wore the skins of wolves, and Lamoral's own ancestors were inventing civilization back in the sunny hills of Lombardy.

Once he'd stepped over the branch, Lamoral reloaded and

snapped the breech shut. Other shots rang through the woods, as did the keepers' calls. The beaters clattered closer. Lamoral moved forward, saw another pig, fired. This one took both barrels before it stopped moving.

Lamoral killed three more pigs in the next ten minutes. Firing was more or less continuous by now. Lamoral was reloading after the last when he saw movement on his left, back behind a clump of bracken. He cautiously raised his gun, his finger still outside the trigger guard, and was thankful for his own caution when he saw, over the simple sight, a man's tufted hat. Someone had strayed off his assigned turf.

The man moved, and Lamoral saw an intent black profile. Edwardes.

Lamoral's mouth went dry. Edwardes shouldn't be here at all.

The singer disappeared behind another clump of fern. Lamoral glanced back over one shoulder, in the direction of civilization, and tried to decide what to do. He could creep back to the starting point and safety, but what if Edwardes weren't looking for him? What if he was stalking Alex, who was the next hunter to Lamoral's left?

This should all be visible to the techs in the VTO. He wondered if they were summoning help.

Lamoral saw violent movement as Edwardes drove his big body through a clump of bushes. The tenor was making a lot of noise: he clearly wasn't used to this. Lamoral could probably track him by ear.

He crouched down low and slipped after. There was a fusillade of shots off on the left. Lamoral found the big man's tracks, followed carefully. Ahead Edwardes loomed, silhouetted for a moment against a white sheet of mist, and then the mist absorbed him.

Lamoral slid forward into a tangle of bracken and waited. Something crunched ahead of him. It sounded as if Edwardes was doubling back. Lamoral raised his gun, softly eased off the safety, put his finger inside the trigger guard. Waited. Ferns waved just ahead. Edwardes was only feet away.

Suddenly, to his astonishment, Lamoral was face-to-face with a huge black sow. His nerves shrieked. His finger twitched on the first trigger, but he stopped himself from firing just in time. The sow gave a squeal of rage and dashed off to the right, beating down ferns as it went.

Lamoral's heart thrashed in his throat. He waited a moment or two while he got his terror under control. Then he crept forward and found himself in a stand of young pine, with Edwardes in plain sight twenty yards away, breathing out mist, his rifle at port arms. The beaters were banging trees with their spears just a short distance away. The hunt was nearly over.

Lamoral put the bushy trunk of a tree between him and Edwardes. It was barely possible, he supposed, that Edwardes was here by accident. He very much wanted to believe that was the case.

Hunting horns rang through the woods. They were calling an end to the shooting: the beaters and huntsmen were getting too close to each other for the shooting to safely continue.

Lamoral put his rifle to his shoulder, but kept the barrels depressed. He had the drop on the man; he'd call out to him and convince him to lower his weapon.

He had to move out around the lower branches of the pine for a clear view, and as he did so Edwardes turned and saw him. Lamoral could see Edwardes' eyes widen with shock; and then the big man threw up his gun and fired.

Lamoral flung himself behind the bole of the tree, onto the ground. Somehow his own gun didn't go off. Edwardes' bullet made a horrible buzzsaw sound as it passed overhead. Edwardes worked the bolt of his rifle and sent another .458 round after the first.

Lamoral could taste dead leaves in his mouth. He crawled back away from the tree, holding his gun carefully so the triggers wouldn't catch on something and fire it off by mistake. He could hear Edwardes crashing through undergrowth out in front of him somewhere.

The keepers were blowing their horns insistently at this break of discipline. The hunt was *over*, dammit! Lamoral found some cover behind a fallen tree and waited. Something wet and cold was seeping through the leather knees of his trousers.

"Lamoral, was that you?"

Edwardes' voice echoed from the trees. Lamoral pointed his rifle in the direction of its likely point of origin.

"Lamoral, I'm sorry I shot at you! We've got to talk!"

The trained voice seemed to be coming from everywhere. Lamoral could hear twigs snapping off on his right. He pointed his gun that way.

"The recording techs are dead!" Edwardes bellowed. "Nobody's seeing this! I didn't mean to shoot at you, Lamoral!"

Damn, it sounded as if the voice was coming from the left. Lamoral swung the muzzles of his gun around, stuck his head up above the fallen tree in hopes of seeing something.

A gun went off, close by. The horrible whizzing sound of a heavy-caliber bullet wailed overhead, seemingly right to the left. Lamoral ducked down, swung his rifle to the right again and saw Alex standing on the edge of a deadfall, silhouetted plainly against a patch of mist, his rifle half-raised. He knew Edwardes couldn't miss seeing Alex if he was standing anywhere nearby.

"Edwardes!" Lamoral shouted, and rose to his feet. Something moved in front of him and he fired both barrels at it, then ducked and ran off to the left. Edwardes popped up right in front of him, not at all where he expected. Edwardes' rifle was raised to his shoulder. Lamoral dived behind a tree, scrabbling at a bed of pine needles as Edwardes' bullet ploughed up dirt two meters away. Lamoral rolled frantically, trying to hang onto his gun; and then there was another shot and the horrid sound of a bullet striking flesh, and as Lamoral rolled out from behind the tree he saw Edwardes dead, fallen back against a stump, arms outflung, a red cavern centered on his massive chest.

Lamoral rose from the bed of needles, his head swimming. Alex stood on his eminence, a wisp rising from his gun-barrel.

"Do you mean to tell me he was trying to kill *you*?" he asked.

Lamoral stared at the body. Words wouldn't come.

Through the trees came the belated thrashing of their rescuers.

* * *

Eurydike had shot two pigs, but the recoil from the Perugini-Visini over-and-under had made her shoulder ache, so she'd returned to the starting point and gone to the VTO to watch the proceedings on video. Once there, she found both techs shot in the head, the pistol lying on the control console next to them, and all the recordings erased. She ran to one of the huntsmen, got him to blow the call that ended the hunt, then rounded up a party to head for the continuing sound of gunfire. Police VTOs flooded the place minutes afterwards.

"It was an old gun that shot the techs," reported the police commissaire. "A Walther P-38. There were no fingerprints on the gun or bullets, but our computers traced the registry to you."

"The pistol was in the gun room," Lamoral said. His breastbone had a hollow, inexplicable ache; he clutched Eurydike to himself as if she were a compress and spoke through a filter of her black hair. "People were in and out all the time, choosing rifles for the hunt; anyone could have taken it."

"We'll have to charge you for being careless with the pistol, then," the commissaire said, making a satisfied note on his portable computer-recorder. He either didn't have the eye/ear implants or lacked Helmsley's style.

"Really, commissaire," said Alex, "they were our *guests*." He was sitting on a fallen tree, watching two policewomen bagging up his rifle in plastic.

"Hospitality," with a businesslike smile, "does not include handing out guns to shoot one another."

"Telephone for you, highness." It was one of the huntsmen. Lamoral took the portable phone and identified himself.

"This is Claudius. Do we start the takeover attempt?"

Lamoral tried to clear his head. Would the public consider this his disaster, or the Set's?

Mary Maude Mullen had allowed two killers into the Set. That would have to be the line.

"Go ahead," he said. "Announce it immediately."

"Not tomorrow? I've already started getting calls from members of the syndicate; they're very nervous."

"Now. Edwardes killed Cao Cao, and he tried to kill me. It's time for some changes."

"Yes. Very well." A sigh. "I'll have to rewrite the press release."

"You'll know the line to take."

"Yes. It will take a few hours or so for the announcement to be ready."

"In the meantime, prod the syndicate to buy. Shares will be dropping."

"Very good."

"I'll be there when I can."

He gave the phone back to the keeper. Eurydike was looking up at him with a puzzled frown.

"What's happening?" she said.

"A proxy fight for control of the Set."

"You picked a hell of a time to start one."

He looked at Alex, the busy police, the rifles wrapped in a miniature version of the plastic sack that contained Edwardes' mortal remains.

"I think I've been in one for a long time," he said.

The takeover bid failed, though it came within an ace of success: Mary Maude Mullen and her board squeaked by after agreeing to more thorough psychological screening and more attention paid to Adjustment. Lamoral and his syndicate retired with grace and greenmail. Everybody made money, and so all was more or less forgotten, if not precisely forgiven.

A few Set-weeks later, Claudius died and was replaced by his son Miguel, a soft-spoken, soft-handed stranger. Two Set-months after that, Miguel "retired"—Lamoral was never clear why, or to what—and was replaced by a fine-boned woman, Marie, who was named after that poetasting ancestress to whom Rilke dedicated his *Elegies*.

And two Set-months after that, Gstaad was reported to be in fashion again, after spending a half-century out of it, and thither went the Party Set for midwinter, to spend the day on the slopes and the night watching bonfires kindled on every peak, like lighthouses for Zeppelins cruising at low altitude, lost and looking for home.

* * *

"How were the slopes?"

Eurydike wasn't at her best on skis; she'd spent the day cutting arabesques across the perfect ice of the skating rink.

"Curiously bare," said Lamoral, "but lovely. I wonder if Set security cleared everybody out."

"There weren't many on the rink, either. Or in this hotel."

"Ratings are up, anyway." Carrying his orange-juice-and-champagne, Lamoral joined her on the low sunken couch around the wood fire. A few other Set people chatted, drifted, drank, waiting for sunset and dinner.

Lamoral took a low, flat box out of his jacket pocket. "A gift," he said.

"Another one? Thank you. I'm really not deserving of all this, you know . . ." Her voice drifted off as she opened the box and saw the star, flashing with diamonds and brilliants, sitting atop its coiled ribbon.

"It's the Order of the Black Eagle and of Skanderbeg," Lamoral said helpfully. "There will have to be a formal investiture later, of course, but I thought you'd like to see it."

She looked at him with a baffled expression. "I didn't know you could give these away."

"I didn't. The presentation will be made by King Sulejman II of Albania and Kosovo. Of course he's only the *pretender* to Kosovo, but . . ."

"Albania?"

"It seems you've done a lot of good works in Albania."

"Albania? I don't remember—"

"Or someone," with a straightfaced smile, "has done them in your name."

Comprehension dawned. "Ah."

"And of course, at the same time, there will be a coronation. You're to be Princess of the Ghegs."

Her eyes narrowed. "Don't the Ghegs, whoever they are, have anything to say about this?"

Lamoral sipped his mimosa. Champagne foamed pleasantly at the base of his tongue. "You're a heroine to the Ghegs, my dear. After all you've done for them, the Dinarics ring with your praises."

"You'll have to remind me sometime what exactly it is I've done."

"After that last earthquake, they've got a lot to be grateful for, believe me. I think making you royalty is the very least you could do."

"Royalty," Eurydike said. Her expression grew grim. "I begin to perceive a purposeful drift in all this. How is the *Almanach de Gotha* going to rate this peerage of mine?"

"Normally," Lamoral said, "they don't rate modern titles highly, but it seems that research has also been done into your forebears."

"I was *assembled*. I don't *have any* . . ."

"On the Apostolidis side, old Basil turns out to have been descended from three Byzantine emperors, notably Alexius I Comnenus, as well as the Ottoman sultan Abdul Hamet I. On the Ichimonji side—well, did you know old Ichiro was from a noble family?"

"He never told me."

"He goes back to the twelfth century. Your ancestors, in fact, are far better than mine. Franz Taxis was just an Italian merchant, after all."

"Down on your knees, peasant swine," she said offhandedly, and then flushed bright red when he did exactly that.

"I realize the Order of the Black Eagle and Skanderbeg is hardly the traditional diamond ring . . ." he began.

"Get up." Turning away. "Don't do this to me."

"Yes, your highness." He rejoined his mimosa and regarded her from over its rim.

"I'll have to think about all of this."

"I believe we'll be seeing Sulejman in a couple of Setdays. You can let him know if you're feeling sufficiently noble."

She looked at him. "This is just a game to you, isn't it?"

"Not entirely."

"You have to win at everything. Everything's tactics, like going up a mountain."

"Or proving a postulate."

Her brows knit. "You can't prove a postulate. It's a given."

"Proving a theorem, then." Irritatedly. "Whatever the hell you prove."

"If you'd won control of the Party Set, would you be so eager to take this tack?"

"We could still be prince and princess. We'd just be royalty here."

"I don't believe we've settled that I'm going to be princess of anything. I don't like getting caught in all this—" Her hands twisted in an invisible mesh. "This web of yours."

"We have nothing but time."

"You haven't left me many choices. Accept everything you've done, or reject it all." She was silent for a moment. "If I reject it, then what?"

"Then I'll make other plans."

"Would I be in them?"

"I don't know."

She put her arms around herself as if warding a chill. "This is all so cold-blooded."

"You wouldn't let me stay on my knees. That's supposed to be the romantic, warm-blooded part."

A half-smile crossed her face. "Okay. You've got me there." She shook her head. "What if the *Almanach de Gotha* decides all these arrangements are just too convenient? What if I'm a second, or third?"

"Didn't I mention . . . ? About a decade ago, my grandniece Marie bought the *Almanach de Gotha* for me. I can write in it what I damn well please."

Eurydike sighed and leaned back on the couch. "You have spun exceeding fine, Lamoral."

"I've had a half-century or more to make my plans. If we drop out of the Set together, we'll live in realtime and you'll get to see me improvise."

She looked at him appraisingly. "I might look forward to that."

"I hope that's grounds for optimism."

"We'll see."

With that, she rose from her couch and strolled across the room to talk to Indira.

The decoration, in its case, was left on the sofa.

Lamoral pocketed it.

* * *

"My new composition," Wayne Unger said, "is called 'l'Amoral.' " He smiled. "With an apostrophe."

Lamoral, without the apostrophe, would just as soon have left the room. Instead he smiled politely and finished his dessert.

Unger's voice rose, embracing his audience. Someone in the know, Lamoral realized, had turned off the dining room's canned music.

> Singular and duplicate,
> A pillar of the ages takes voice—
> Or is it the engendering ages
> Who speak with such careful circumspection?
> *(And the mountain stands beyond ethics.)*
>
> Contriving his conquests
> With rope and peg, the world
> A rockface to be mounted, scarred
> With the brutal crampons of ascent.
> *(And the mountain stands outside of time.)*
>
> Boar: a record kill today—
> And so die all pretenders!
> The brittle phalange of the Reaper crooks
> To those who stand too near.
> *(And the mountain stands forever.)*
>
> The mountain is his protoplast.
> His zygote has the germ of eminence.
> But the mountain is rimed by frost.
> And the mountain kills with a shrug.
> *(And the mountain stands . . .)*

Carolly applauded briskly; Alex laughed so hard he almost slid under his table. Eurydike, across the table from Lamoral, gnawed her lip.

"I believe I'll have some more coffee," said Lamoral.

The waiter poured. Unger loomed closer. "Like it?" he said.

Lamoral thought for a moment. "I think you mixed your

metaphor, Unger. I can't *climb* a mountain if I *am* a mountain, now can I?''

''I'd like to think of my metaphors as expandable.''

''And I believe rime is salt and has nothing to do with frost.''

Unger's face beamed delight. ''Poetic license, dear boy!''

''Face it, Lamoral,'' called Kitsune gaily from the next table. ''Unger's got your number.'' She had, to everyone's surprise, pre-empted Alex by tossing his shoes before he could toss hers, and had taken up with a new Set member Tait Singh, leaving Alex uncharacteristically bereft of a companion.

''I'll work on it,'' Unger said. He patted Lamoral's shoulder. ''I'll make it better. It was just an improvisation, after seeing Les Diablerets and the Wildhorn from the Dart this afternoon.''

''I'll look forward to the next version. Though I'm no real judge of-poetry.''

''Come now. You inherited Rilke, after all.''

''So I did.'' Lamoral sipped coffee. ''If you want more inspiration, go look at a real killer mountain. Tell your Dart to get you a close look at the North Face of the Eiger. That's out by Grindelwald.''

''That's one of yours, isn't it?''

''Mine and Alex's.''

''Of course.'' Condescendingly. ''Of course.''

Radiating satisfaction, Unger headed in the direction of the bar. Lamoral called after him. ''Are you going to do the Doyenne next?''

He saw, out of the corner of his vision, that Kitsune's eyes widened with interest. He smiled inwardly: if he planted that harpoon well enough, Unger might well have to perform.

He looked at Eurydike.

''Have you been talking to him?''

''Unger?'' She shook her head. ''No. Not recently.''

''Your thoughts seem to be running in parallel.''

Eurydike fiddled with her teaspoon. ''Some opinions concerning you can be held in common.''

''Am I growing that predictable? I should do something startling and break up the stereotype.''

"Perhaps you should."

"What I would like to do, at the moment, is to take my coffee onto the terrace and enjoy the view. But people would assume I was leaving the room because I'm angry at Unger."

She looked at him curiously. "*Are* you angry at Unger?"

"Yes."

"Then why should you care if people know it?"

He sighed. "You're correct, of course. Will you join me?"

"Certainly."

Steam rose from their coffee, plumed from their noses. The fires atop Vanil Noir and the other peaks and prominences wouldn't be lit till midnight, and the valley was dark. Brittle starlight gleamed off high snowfields, and low-lying clouds stroked the slopes like cats rubbing themselves against someone's leg. Lamoral absorbed it all for a long, long moment.

He was aware of Eurydike watching him. He turned to her.

"So what happened up there?" He knew the *up there*, another mountain on the other side of the world.

"Changabang."

"Yes."

"I always thought Changabang sounded silly if you don't know what it means. Shining Mountain. Because it's white, and the other Himalayas are dark."

"I sense an elision coming on."

Lamoral gazed bleakly into the dark. "It was a stupid accident," he said. "If it weren't for a lot of wild coincidences, no one would have got hurt." Lamoral could taste it, the sudden jolt of fear, the swirl of vertigo, the urge to curl up and protect his head and neck, the final impact at the end . . .

"We hadn't got very far up the mountain, and the accident happened low down," he said. "A little over nineteen thousand feet. A place full of overhangs—Boardman and Tasker, who were the first up the West Wall in 1976, called it the Toni Kurz pitch, after a man who died on a similar place on the Eiger. Alex went first, working his way out under this overhang, and I was belaying him. Karl-August was below me, picking up surplus pitons so we could reuse them. He was attached to another line altogether. Alex planted a peg under this giant overhang, put a running belay on it, then worked his way around the other side and up. He was out of my sight, but that wasn't unusual. Once he got around the overhang he planted an ice piton there, in some old black ice that had been sitting there since the dawn of time, and shouted for me to follow.

"I went out along the rope with a jumar—it's this ratchetlike thing that attaches you to the rope, so you can follow the pioneer and not worry about falling off. But when Alex went off ahead he left his pack with me so that he'd have more freedom to get up that difficult pitch, and I was carrying my own pack as well, so that meant that between the two packs I weighed about forty kilos more than he did, and that first peg under the overhang just pulled right out—it supported Alex all right, but not me.

"And *that* normally would have been okay, because the line was still pegged on either end, except that it wasn't—" Lamoral paused, trying to figure out a way to explain it. "When I was jumaring after him, Alex decided he didn't like the looks of his last peg, so he gave it a final tug, and it tore right out of that old rotten ice. So he quickly drove in another peg in a more secure place, and detached himself from the line and clipped himself to the new peg, and he was right on the verge of clipping the line to the new peg when I tore the *other* peg out of the rock face, and my weight ripped the line right out of Alex's hands . . . so now there was nothing supporting me on that end, and I fell."

Eurydike watched him, her face in shadow. "Were you hurt?"

"No. The pegs on the other end held, and I was wearing a helmet. I dropped about twenty meters and then the line caught me. I swung like a pendulum across the rock face, and I balled myself up. At the end of my swing I hit Karl-August. I hit him with my helmet, and the force of it broke his back. He died a few hours later."

There was a moment of silence, then Eurydike let out a long sigh. Lamoral realized she'd been holding her breath.

"How did Alex get down?" she asked.

"Getting down mountains is a lot easier than getting up. Once he was above the overhangs, all he had to do was drive

in some pitons and abseil down to where I was, using one of
the other ropes he was carrying. He and I were both with
Karl-August at the end.'' Lamoral looked up at Vanil Noir
and thought of leaving Karl-August behind, mummied in his
sleeping bags and hanging from a half-dozen lines, swaying
in the wind below the Toni Kurz pitch until someone could
come in a VTO and bring home the body. Lamoral had cut
the Austrian flag Karl-August wore on his outer jacket and
carried it back as a remembrance. ''All I had was a stiff neck
from the impact,'' he said. ''I walked around in a collar for
a month. That was all.''

''I've never seen anyone die.'' Eurydike shivered. ''I ran
out on the war, then joined the Set. Edwardes' was the only
body I've ever seen.''

''They do seem to collect around me.'' Grimly. ''Unger
was right about that.''

''And I ran out on the implications of my own work. I
could see what was going to happen once we worked out the
n-dimensional business, and I didn't want to deal with it. I
badly wanted to be someplace else.''

He looked at her in surprise. ''What are the implications,
then?''

She hesitated, then shook her head. ''You wouldn't believe
me.''

Eurydike put her coffee down on the rail, stepped up to
him, put her arms around him. Her head nestled against his
shoulder.

Another body, Lamoral thought. He was thankful this one
was warm.

Up high the beacons were leaping from peak to peak, like
alarums out of Walter Scott. The Party Set hung on the terrace, gazing up, watching the fires in silence.

On the other end of the building, under the pale floodlights
of the skating rink, elevated on one blade tip, Eurydike spun
slowly, her chin sweeping perilously close to the ice. Lamoral watched and warmed himself with a glass of brandy.
A bugzapper sat on a table nearby, driving off eavesdroppers.

She straightened; her other blade touched ice. Eurydike
pushed off, came slowly toward him.

"I've decided something," she said.

"So have I."

She smiled. "You first."

"I've decided that elisions are out for the season. I'm going to climb Changabang."

"Good. Evasions are going out with elisions. I've decided that I'm going to be Princess of the Ghegs."

"I'm pleased for you."

"The Party Set was another way of running away. I'm done with that."

He kissed her, then lowered his voice. "I've likewise decided that I'm not making the climb a Party Set event. I want to do it quietly. It's not for popular consumption, it's just something I want to do. The Party Set can find out about it afterward."

She looked at him carefully. "Is Alex going up with you?"

"That's up to him."

"Not to hear him tell it."

Lamoral smiled. "You can't *make* someone climb a mountain. Alex likes to complain, but he's really a very good mountaineer. Better than me, actually."

Eurydike was amused. "For once you and he agree on something."

"I'm a fairly dull climber. Very organized, very logical, very proper. Alex is lazy and careless about some things, like making correct bivouacs or cooking meals, but on the rock face he can get inspired. He's done things that would have terrified me, and done them brilliantly."

"He's never struck me as the nerves-of-steel type."

Lamoral gave a ritual sigh. "He's got a lot of fine characteristics, but he's never applied himself properly."

"Cliché, Lamoral."

"Cliché, but true. To be a noble younger son is to be a cliché, and that is unfortunate."

She put her arm on his. "Then we'll only have one son, Lamoral. The rest, daughters."

"Whatever you say," smiling, "your highness."

"The Party Set has bagged its second royal."

"Say rather," another wag, "it's created its first!"

The Party Set was delighted with Eurydike's investiture— along with the Nobel, she was providing excuses for the Party Set to be spontaneous, and anyway reasons to visit Albania were few. The festivities were delightful, and Eurydike's bodyguard of Ghegs, with their red hats, mustachios, and antique, much-loved Lee-Enfields, had the proper resonance of color and menace. Afterwards, as the Set went off to its cold bunkers, Eurydike, Lamoral, and Alex flew to Regensburg.

Alex had agreed to the climb with surprising lack of fuss. Perhaps Kitsune's rejection had left him feeling at loose ends. Eurydike had been ennobled in mid-August, and Lamoral planned for a month's climbing and conditioning in Bavaria, moving to India in mid-September, making a long hike to the base of Changabang to accustom himself and Alex to the altitude, then beginning the assault on Changabang around the first of October. The schedule would give about two weeks to climb the mountain before the monsoon arrived and made the whole thing impossible.

Research was done into modern mountaineering techniques. Some were useful—laminated polymerized crampons, built into the boot and spring-loaded, which not only got rid of the tedious business of taking them on and off but eliminated the problem of a metal crampon conducting cold into the boot. Some of the new techniques were useful, but declined: self-contained n-dimension bivouacs, containing food, clothing, heat, and beds, struck Lamoral as decadent.

Lamoral and Alex hiked and climbed throughout the day. They had the forests and mountains almost to themselves. Even Regensburg seemed to have few people on the streets.

"People are leaving," Maria said. "There is much opportunity elsewhere."

"Where?"

A shrug. "Off the planet." Lamoral had the feeling she didn't particularly care.

They climbed in solitude. Lamoral began to enjoy the isolation of the slopes. He remembered the Alps as being packed with climbers.

"Your schedule doesn't leave much room for error," said

Alex, looking at his pocket calendar. He was perched on the desk in Lamoral's office in the old monastery, surrounded by pictures of mountains. Eurydike half-reclined on an old chair in the corner, reading an ancient magazine.

"Einmal jedes," Lamoral said, *"nur einmal. Einmal und nichtmehr."* Eurydike frowned, mentally translating. Just once, everything, only for once. Once and no more.

Rilke, of course.

Alex looked at Lamoral quizzically. "This makes *twice*, Lamoral." Eurydike laughed.

"We haven't climbed it yet. We're only going to do that once."

"Whatever you say."

"I'm taking something of Karl-August's with me. I'm going to leave it up there."

Alex nodded. "I like that."

"Vidcom for you, sir." The voice of a footman came out of the intercom.

The caller was a dark-skinned man with a clipped mustache and a military uniform. "I am Squadron Leader Daram-Louis Ram, your serene highness. I wished to speak to you regarding your application to climb Changabang."

Lamoral aimed a pleased look at Alex. "I am at your service, squadron leader."

"The Government of the Southwest Asian Coalition is pleased to grant your application, your highness. I have been assigned as your liaison officer."

"In that case, please call me Lamoral."

The officer grinned. "Call me Louis, then."

"We were hoping to fly into Lata next month, and walk to Changabang from there."

"That will be suitable. If you will inform me of the date, I will meet you there." Louis looked at Lamoral carefully. "Sir," he said, "I am rated an expert climber. I would like to accompany you up the West Wall."

Lamoral's eyes flicked to Alex, who shook his head, then back to the screen. "I don't know how possible that is," he said.

"I have been up Changabang before, though we went up the Southwest Ridge, not the West Face. I have also been to the top of Everest, climbed the South Face of Annapurna, and have made two attempts at K-2." Louis smiled. "Those, alas, were not blessed by success."

"I'm impressed, Louis," Lamoral said. "But I'll have to consult with the other half of my expedition." Alex, perched behind the comm unit, was still vigorously shaking his head.

"Much depends on chemistry," Louis said. "I understand that."

"And we plan to make a classical ascent. No radios, no television, no bivouacking in the nth dimension. And we carry all supplies from the base camp on our backs. No porters once we begin, no caching stuff from a VTO."

"I would be most enthusiastic to agree to those conditions, Lamoral."

Lamoral began to have a good feeling about the man. "I'll be in touch, then."

"I will be looking forward."

"I don't like it," Alex said. "I thought this was going to be just the two of us."

Eurydike looked at them from over her magazine. "What exactly do you need an elision officer for, anyway?"

Lamoral swiveled his chair. "The Indian—Southwest Asian—government insists on it. He's there to make certain we don't break any laws and that we climb the mountain that we're supposed to."

Eurydike seemed amused. "Is that a problem?"

"Sometimes. Nanda Devi's been closed for a couple centuries at least, and we're going to be just in the next valley."

"Why?"

"Because Nanda Devi is holy—she's not just a mountain, she's a goddess. In addition to the Indian Army, she's guarded by seven rishis who live in the Rishi Ganga, and her Sanctuary has been off-limits for a very long time. Pilgrims walk hundreds of miles to get a glimpse of her."

Eurydike seemed amused. "You weren't planning on sneaking up Nanda Devi while no one was looking, were you?"

"And drive every Hindu and Buddhist fanatic into a homicidal rage? No, thank you."

"We never saw Nanda Devi on our former journey," Alex added. "She was hidden in cloud the entire time."

Lamoral thought about that. "The Goddess turned her back on us that trip."

Alex was silent. Eurydike watched them with interest.

Lamoral swiveled his chair toward his computer. "Let's find out about this Daram-Louis," he said.

What he discovered was impressive. The officer was only 26 and had been on a major climbing expedition every year since he was 17. He'd been the only survivor of the advance party on the first K2 expedition, and gone on to attempt the mountain again the next year, when bad weather drove him back just short of the summit.

"Looks as if he's good."

"He won't be Karl-August," said Alex.

Which was perfectly true.

At noon the clouds streamed away like something in a fast-motion video, and the sun blazed off the white granite fang of the Shining Mountain. The increase in brightness gave an almost hallucinatory quality to the 17,000-foot meadow where they had pitched their tents—each grass spear was sharply outlined, each wildflower a ball of flame. Changabang's snaking plume of snow, old monsoonfall torn off its horns by 60-knot winds, gleamed like powdered silver. Lamoral could see a VTO threading the gap between Kalanka and the Rishi Kot like a shining needle, and knew it was Eurydike coming with their supplies.

In the old days they would have had to hire dozens of porters to trek the stuff in. It was lucky the VTOs could land on the Base Camp's meadow: aside from Louis, Lamoral hadn't seen a single human being since his arrival in India, not even in Lata, not even a hermit or a pilgrim on his way to the Goddess. Maybe, he thought, they flew to the Sanctuary in giant aerial buses. Even the bugzappers hadn't found a hidden camera or microphone since leaving Albania.

Clouds still wrapped Nanda Devi, a shroud of darkness on the otherwise bright horizon. Lamoral turned his eyes away from it. He did not want to assign any import to those clouds.

Louis was melting snow for their luncheon of fruit drink

and porridge. Lamoral walked farther out onto the silver-edged grass and gestured for Alex to join him.

"Louis is going to have to join us," he said.

"Damn it, Lamoral!"

"He's good. He's amiable, even when you're being unpleasant, and he's walked all these miles with us from Lata and made our life a lot easier by doing most of the actual work."

"Yes, I'll concede that. But he's—I don't know—gone away somewhere most of the time. He's drifting."

"He seems to be efficient enough when he's actually doing something. *I'm* not going to tell him he can't climb."

"Don't I have a say in this?"

"Yes. But if you tell him, make sure you tell him it's your decision alone, that it's your refusal, not ours, not mine."

Alex's bearded face was sullen. "Damn you anyway. Everything's always got to be arranged your way."

"Here's Eurydike." Turning away.

He knew Alex would never tell Louis on his own.

The VTO came to a landing on a bed of starry, violet flowers. Eurydike had brought, from Schloss St. Emmeram, an old chased-silver flask full of coffee. She poured for herself and Lamoral, but the boiling point was so low at this altitude that half of it steamed away before they could drink. The remains were so strong as to be unpalatable.

Eurydike tasted and made a face. "I brought a picnic lunch for four," she said. "At least *that* won't boil away."

"Fresh vegetables, I hope."

She stepped out from the lee of the VTO and winced in the sudden light of Changabang. "That's the one you're going up, isn't it?"

"It's the only white mountain here."

"It's vertical!"

Lamoral smiled. "That's rather the point." He pointed, one by one, at the other peaks. "Purbi Dunagiri. Dunagiri. Rishi Pahar, Hardeol, Tursuli. Rishi Kot, where the demigods live. Hunaman the Monkey God. Kalanka the Destroyer."

"I hope these names aren't to be taken literally."

"I hope so, too." There was a boom and Eurydike gave

a little jump. She turned and saw a white lace curtain dropping with infinite grace down Changabang's face, its edges curling in the tearing winds.

"Avalanche?" she said.

"Yes. But there's not much snow in it. Changabang's so steep it doesn't collect snow for long."

She looked at him sharply. "Is that supposed to be a consolation?"

"It's not a life-threatening avalanche. We could hang on very well through something like that. And have. I'm a lot more worried about rocks."

She looked around the meadow, the late flowers dancing between the white arms of glaciers. "I keep thinking what the Party Set would turn this into. White tablecloths, servants in turbans, an orchestra, a special surprise appearance by a famous yogi . . ."

"And Unger would write another damned poem about snow." He looked at her. "One doesn't want that, does one?"

"No. I'm relieved they're not here."

"You've lived outside the Set for two months. How do you find it?"

"Lonely." Her expression was disturbed. "There's no one out there. The whole planet has been largely depopulated, and most of those left are . . . not at home, somehow. Pleasant, polite, but absent. Like your grand-niece."

Lamoral thought about Louis. The Indian climber fit the description as well: harmless, pleasant, but somehow lacking, despite his record, the cold gritty edge of determination he had come to expect from serious climbers.

" 'I have lost my passion,' " Lamoral said, " 'why should I need to keep it Since what is kept must be adulterated?' "

"What was that?"

"*Gerontion.* A favorite of Unger's. I was wondering aloud if perhaps the human race has lost all its passion."

She shuddered. "That would make us—the Set—the last of the old breed."

"One wonders why they'd find us interesting. Yet out ratings are up."

"My thoughts of retirement from the Set never included taking up residence among somnambulists."

"After the climb we'll do some exploration. Of the humans around us."

Eurydike grimaced. "Either the Party Set or taking up residence in early Eliot. Not a choice I relish."

" 'More than ever the things we live with are falling away.' "

Eurydike grinned. "You've got to stop quoting Rilke every time you need something profound to say. People will think you unoriginal."

"They've never thought that of Unger."

"Let's have our picnic."

"Let's."

That night the VTO rose into the night, its brief fires flickering off Changabang's horns. *The hardness of life,* Lamoral thought, *the long experience of love . . . but then, under the stars, what then? the more deeply untellable stars?*

The Shining Mountain stood, like one of the *Elegies'* titanic, unknowable Angels, above the meadow.

Tomorrow they would begin to climb it.

The final morning they woke at five and warmed snow to cook their breakfast porridge. At dawn they left their tents and bags behind on the ledge, made a long, horizontal, slightly ascending traverse, and jumared up a long groovelike crack pioneered the afternoon before. Afterwards was a long free climb, no more pegs or fixed ropes, just the one rope the three shared between them. The last 300 meters were right in the mountain's plume, the 50-knot wind flinging in their faces a million ice crystals, little stinging rainbows.

And then they stepped out of the plume and were at the same instant on the summit. It was two in the afternoon. The journey had taken 11 days, most consumed in portering their supplies in relays up the lower slopes.

Lamoral was too tired to spend much time in congratulating himself. He triggered his helmet camera to take some pictures, the only ones he'd taken, and all for the sole purpose of proving they'd been there—he considered there were already too many pictures of exhausted, grinning climbers stupidly waving ice axes on one summit or another.

Only now did he remember to look at the view. To the east he could see into Nepal, a line of white crests stretching away forever; and away north, past Kalanka and Purbi Dunagiri, the mountain peaks marched off into Tibet. There was a clouded darkness there creeping over the ridges, signalling a storm that would probably strike Changabang about midnight.

Lamoral didn't look toward Nanda Devi. He knew its twin peaks were still covered in cloud.

Louis was singing a prayer and scattering candy for the gods. Alex was lost in the view. Lamoral opened a pocket on his overcoat and took out something he'd prepared, a small stone he'd picked up in the Alps wrapped in an Austrian flag, the one Karl-August Hormayr had on his jacket when he died.

What was Austria now? A district in the European Union, last he'd heard, but that had been decades ago. Before the war. Perhaps by now Austria, or the Union, was one with the Nineveh and Tyre.

Alex was looking restless.

Lamoral buried the flag in the snow, then stood for a moment and looked at the whiteness and failed entirely to think of something profound to say or do.

Time to go down. Lamoral cleaned the ice out of his crampons—metal ones would have been worn to nubbins by now—and began his descent. As it was, they would probably not reach the bivouac before dark.

Descending through the plume was worrying, stepping cautiously downhill with only limited visibility. One mistake on someone's part could drag all three off a precipice. But soon they were out of the plume and plunging down through the snow like schoolboys. After that was a careful Alpine descent that took them to the top of the fixed ropes and the long crack that dropped them down a significant fraction of the West Wall.

"I'm feeling fit," Alex said. "I'll go last and pick up the ropes."

Lamoral looked at him. In spite of the little fuel cell that fed refined oxygen inside the face mask of Lamoral's helmet, he was panting for breath. "Are you sure?"

"Just have a nice hot drink waiting for me at Camp Three."

"I'll do that."

Louis went first, his bright yellow helmet disappearing down the long, cold gully; and then Lamoral retracted his laminated crampons, clipped on his descendeur, and followed. Halfway down the groove was a bend that snaked around an overhang—a nasty little 500-kilo flake that seemed to be held to the mountainside only by a couple of patches of thin, black, primeval ice. Lamoral carefully avoided touching the flake on his way down, not wanting to drop it on Louis's head.

Lamoral could see Louis waiting on the ledge at the bottom of the gulley, faceplate up, munching a piece of chocolate and enjoying the view. There was hammering from above—maybe Alex was putting in a more secure peg.

And then Lamoral felt something through his line—a vibration, a tautening, something *not right*—and he looked up to see the half-ton flake coming down.

"Rock!" he yelled, and jumped to one side, swinging clear out of the gully—suddenly, with the flake gone, there was more slack in the rope—and the flake bounded past in a chaos of snow and rattling black pebble-ice. Lamoral smashed onto the rock face at the end of his swing and, bouncing back into the gully, saw Louis look up just in time to perceive the stone that killed him.

Lamoral could hear crashes as the flake continued its progress down the West Wall. The gully was full of rushing rubble that bounced off Lamoral's shoulders and helmet. Lamoral ignored it and dropped to where Louis was lying, his body still harnessed to the rope.

Dead, of course, his head caved in.

Which, Lamoral perceived, revealed the machinery within.

His mouth went dry. He clipped a karabiner to the next line, the one that made the long descending traverse, unfixed his descendeur from the vertical line, and bent to examine the body.

Daram-Louis Ram was not human. The flesh was real

enough, but what was beneath was all metal alloy bones, bright plastic tendons, silver circuitry.

Ein jeder Engel ist schrecklich.

Boots scrabbled above him. Lamoral looked up and saw Alex coming down, looking over his shoulder.

"Are you all right? That flake—"

"Louis is dead."

"Damn."

Alex braked about five meters above Lamoral's head. He took off one mitten, revealing the heavy glove underneath, then opened his jacket and began feeling for something inside.

Lamoral searched for words. "There's something wrong here, Alex."

Alex took out a small pistol, cocked it, pointed it in Lamoral's direction.

Lamoral let go of the mountain and jumped straight back.

Next thing he knew he was upside-down and moving very rapidly. The rock face scraped the hell out of him even through his heavy clothes. He was only clipped to the line by the one karabiner and his body bouncing against the mountain was more of a brake than the single ring. If Alex fired he didn't hear it.

Lamoral came to a jarring stop at a peg, one placed halfway along the traverse. Somewhat to his surprise, none of his equipment broke.

Lamoral reached for the rope, tilted himself upright. He could feel blood running down his knees and elbows. Off on his right, about 20 meters, he saw Alex making a far more controlled descent to the ledge. Alex needed both hands to control his equipment and had put the pistol away.

But not for long, Lamoral presumed. He clipped his descendeur onto the next length of line and kicked off.

This time there really was a shot. The bullet whizzed off rock, and then Alex was out of sight behind a bulge of white granite.

The rope ended at the next peg. Lamoral was at their previous night's bivouac. Lamoral fixed himself to the next rope, then unclipped the first rope from its peg and let it fall.

Let Alex bridge *that* one.

The dangling rope began to zoom upward quickly. Evidently Alex was on the length between the middle peg and the shelf, and his weight was dragging the now-loose rope through the karabiner on the peg. It wouldn't come free: the rope was knotted at both ends to prevent just that. Alex wouldn't fall; he'd just have a long jumar back up to the ledge.

That gave Lamoral time to pack a tent, a pair of sleeping bags, and some rations. He kicked the rest of the gear over the edge—a straight drop of almost a thousand feet to the icefield below—then abseiled down the next line, unknotted the doubled rope and collected it.

The next abseil took him out of the sun. It was going to be dark and cold very soon. Lamoral thought about it as he collected the next rope.

Alex had no sleeping gear or other supplies: he'd have to spend the night on the mountain, and there was a storm coming on. Even though there were heating elements in his climbing suit, he'd probably be frozen to the rock face by dawn.

There was, however, a tent at Camp Two, on the icefield below. If Alex could reach that he could survive.

All this assumed that Alex wasn't like Louis, that he wasn't made out of machinery that could survive very well in the storm that was coming.

Lamoral suspected he was. Alex had been replaced, like Louis, and when Lamoral discovered Louis' secret, Alex tried to kill him.

The problem of who had done the replacing could wait.

The wind was picking up. The air was full of spindrift and Lamoral was beginning to shiver. He couldn't feel his toes at all. He turned on the heating units in his climbing suit, gloves, and boots.

Lamoral began his next abseil while trying to decide what to do. He still hadn't made up his mind at the bottom, so he retrieved the rope and threw it over the edge—the two he carried were quite enough for getting down the mountain.

It was getting very dark. If the mountain itself hadn't been white he couldn't have seen where he was putting his feet.

That last abseil had taken him to the bottom of the series

of fixed ropes. From here he could reach the ice field in a few easy abseils, and from there it was a long march down the middle third of the mountain, after which another set of fixed ropes would aid his descent to Camp One.

He fixed his anchor for the next abseil, then flung a doubled rope out into the darkness and began his descent. Near the bottom there was a convenient ledge; he paused here, retrieved the rope, and started driving a pair of pitons for another anchor.

"Hey, Lamoral!"

The sound of Alex's voice scared him witless. In an instant he was standing with his back to the rock face, ice axe poised.

"Don't worry, I can't see you. I think I'm over to your right, on the other side of that overhang. Remember that dead-end chimney you pioneered? I abseiled down it. It was an impossible way up, but a very fast way down."

Alex's voice was a shout against the rising wind. Lamoral raised his faceplate and looked frantically left and right. Blown snow stung his face. He began to hear the sound of hammering.

"Bet I can make it to Camp Two before you can!" Cheerfully.

Lamoral tried to decide whether or not it would be wise to reply. In the end he decided it didn't matter. Alex couldn't get to him without giving him plenty of time to react.

"What are you?"

Alex's voice stayed buoyant. "Not a very successful murderer, it would seem. I keep hitting everyone but you!"

Vertigo eddied through Lamoral. He gripped the rock face.

"What do you mean?"

The hammering paused. "Karl-August. Cao Cao. Edwardes. Now poor Louis. I never meant to hit any of them." Alex sounded aggrieved. "You have the devil's own luck, Lamoral. Always have had. If this goes on I'll have to kill off half our acquaintance."

If this was a machine, Lamoral thought, it was doing a damn good job of imitating Alex's style.

"Edwardes was trying to warn you, you know. *He* knew he wasn't the killer, whatever you thought. But he got drunk and overslept, and made it to the hunt late. He found you tracking him, and thought you were me, and took a shot at you. And *I* was tracking you also, hoping to shoot you with a pistol that had Unger's fingerprints all over the magazine— I saw him handling it the previous night. So I found myself having to save your life in order to preserve my neck. And the stupid police never found the extra gun on me.''

''You killed the techs.''

''For God's sake! I didn't want anything recorded, did I?'' In a tone used to explain things to simpletons.

Lamoral turned to face the rock and peered upward, blinking snow off his lashes. He was losing feeling in his nose.

''Why are you doing this?'' he said. Reaching upward, testing a handgrip.

''For strictly hedonistic reasons, of course. I want the money and the title. *And* all twenty-three castles.''

''Perhaps we could reach an accommodation.'' Lamoral pulled his balaklava up over his mouth and nose, then lifted himself up by the handgrip. He wished he hadn't retrieved the damned rope.

''Come on, Lamoral! It's a little late to be bought off. And I'm tired of your gifts anyway—the Set most of all.'' Alex's hammering resumed.

Lamoral reached for another handgrip, pulled himself up, found another, pulled. ''I think there might be reason for an alliance between us,'' he said. ''Did you see Louis' body?''

The hammering paused again. ''Contrary to what you might think,'' Alex said, ''I don't *enjoy* killing people, I just do it when it seems necessary. I've got better things to do than look at corpses.''

Lamoral found a crack above him, stuck his wrist in it, and made a fist. Hauled himself up again. ''Louis wasn't human,'' he said.

Alex seemed at a loss for a reply, then burst out laughing. ''That's just what I tried to tell you!''

''I'm serious. He was some kind of machine.''

''Even if true, which I doubt, I don't see that it alters the relationship between us.''

Lamoral halted, panting for breath. ''There may not be any humans left, outside the Set. What are the titles and lands going to mean then?''

"One Setman more or less isn't going to make much difference in that case, is he?" Cheerfully. Alex went back to hammering.

Lamoral continued his upward climb. Seventy-knot gusts tore at his clothing. He'd thought he'd managed to get above the overhang, but visibility was so low he couldn't be certain. He leaned out into the wind and looked carefully at the rock face to his right.

The hammering came to an end. Lamoral could barely hear Alex's voice. "Race you to Camp Two?"

Lamoral reached out to his right, fingers probing at the rock face.

"No?" Alex seemed disappointed. "We could have a jolly time chasing each other around the ice field in this wind. It's going to be interesting, seeing which one of us gets to Base Camp and the radio first. Are you going to camp tonight, or are you going to try a descent?"

Lamoral reached off to his right again, found a handjam, stuck his fist in it. He began groping rightward with his foot.

"Perhaps you've already gone down?" Alex said.

There was nowhere for Lamoral to set his right foot. He took a breath, then let go with his left hand and foot. He swung out at the end of his jammed right hand, boots scrabbling at the rockface. He found a ledge half a centimeter wide and glazed with ice. Carefully he put weight on it. It seemed willing to support him.

"You're either trying to steal a march on me," Alex said, "or you're playing some kind of game. Either way, I'm leaving."

There was a pause. Lamoral committed himself to the ledge, unjammed his hand, and groped right again.

"*Au revoir!*" Alex sounded suspicious. Lamoral found another handhold and edged right.

He heard no more from Alex. He kept spidering right and eventually got into the dead-end chimney that Alex had abseiled down. Lamoral's face was completely numb. He put down his faceplate and let the helmet fill up with warm oxygen.

He'd gone up this chimney two days before, only to find that the route was completely closed by overhangs, rotten ice, and crumbling rockface. He'd turned back and the party had gone up by another route.

Now Lamoral went down, moving as fast as he could. The wind wasn't as bad but the chimney was full of spindrift and the rocks edged with ice. He tried not to think of clever Alex, suspicious Alex, waiting with his pistol just below him, at the bottom of the chimney.

Lamoral was at the bottom before he expected it and had no time to experience relief before he saw Alex's anchor, the three pitons that held his doubled abseiling rope in their slings.

He could see that there was still weight on the line. He found the point where the line was at its maximum strain, right as it went over the edge of the cliff. He took his ice axe out of its scabbard, raised it and let it fall.

Lamoral spent the night in his tent in the chimney, sleeping vertically in two sleeping bags and pegged down by no less than eight pitons. The storm blew itself out about seven o'clock.

He found Alex's body sprawled on the icefield, where it had created an architecturally perfect drift. Alex had hit the rock face enough on the way down to provide a visual certainty that he died perfectly human.

Lamoral glanced up from the body and saw the bright peaks of Nanda Devi, looking down at him like a pair of towering angels.

King Sulejman was a short man, portly and mustached, with a decided resemblance to his distant and unmemorable ancestor King Zog. In spite of the cold in Schloss Worth's deep freeze, he was sweating when he stepped out. He mopped his forehead with a lace handkerchief.

"Yes," he said. "Terrible."

Lamoral reached into his pocket and removed a pistol. Eurydike, likewise armed, covered Sulejman from the doorway. "You will step in front of my portable x-ray machine, if you please," Lamoral said.

X-rays revealed that Sulejman seemed to have no mechanical parts beyond a few dental implants. Lamoral put his pistol away. Eurydike, pointedly, did not.

"We need to talk," Lamoral said.

Sulejman mopped his forehead again. "Yes. We do."

Lamoral took his guest to the library. Schloss Worth, near Regensburg, was one of his smaller castles; he'd given his servants, most of whom he suspected of being mechanical, the day off.

The Indian Air Force was still scouring Changabang for a pair of bodies that Lamoral had taken good care would never be found. He had told them of a plausible accident in a location far away from any real tragedies.

The smell of old leather and fine paper enveloped them. The King sat in a green leather chair. Lamoral perched on an old oak table in front of him. Eurydike stood to one side, scowled at the Pretender to Kosovo, and kept her hand on her pistol.

"What happened," she said, "to the human race?"

Sulejman looked at her over his shoulder and ventured a nervous smile. "Nothing untoward. We haven't been invaded, if that's what you were suspecting."

"So where is everyone?"

"It's your fault, really. They're off in the nth dimension. In their pocket universes."

"Doing what?" Lamoral asked.

Sulejman shrugged. "Doing whatever they please. Pocket universes can be constructed to the most stringent specifications. It's become quite an art form. And it doesn't take much energy from our universe to create a cascade of creation in the higher dimensions. Our *own* universe may have started with a single particle, and the hyperdimensional universes are similar. Time can be significantly speeded up. One can journey for centuries—millenia, really—in a pocket universe, then return to Earth to discover only a day has passed." Sulejman looked up. "May I smoke?"

"Certainly."

The King lit up. "People are off having adventures. In their own and their friends' creations. Living in alternative timelines, being deities, living lives of self-discovery." Sulejman smiled. "Quite a few have chosen to live in the Party Set. You should be proud."

"And in the meantime, what's happened to Earth?"

"It's—" Sulejman searched for words. "It's the control," he said. "It's become a nexus reality. A station at which all the tracks of alternate realities converge."

"And the Party Set?"

"Another control. This one for humans."

"The Party Set is the control? In other words, we've become the norm?"

Sulejman shrugged. "Most people have been off populating their own universes for subjective eons. I don't know how many of them approach the human norm anymore. It would be nice to have a breeding population should it prove necessary."

Lamoral laughed. "The Doyenne has always thought of us as her pack of dogs. Now the rest of the world plans to keep us around for breeding purposes. She'd be pleased to know how prescient she was."

"Though," Eurydike added, "she wouldn't like her Set being considered anyone's norm."

"The Doyenne doesn't know," Sulejman shrugged. "Who are you to disillusion her?"

Lamoral considered shooting Sulejman then and there. Alex had schemed and murdered for over a century to be the Fifteenth Prince von Thurn und Taxis, and had died without ever knowing that he could have been Galactic Emperor in some alternate reality tailored just for him.

Perhaps perceiving Lamoral's feelings, Sulejman shifted uneasily in his seat, his eyes on the pocket with the gun.

"How long has this been going on?" Lamoral asked.

"Extensively, only a few decades. Once the technology was available, it spread very widely."

Eurydike looked at Lamoral. "I told you, Lamoral. I told you that I didn't want to consider the implications of my own work. Now you know why."

Lamoral held Sulejman's eyes. "And the automata?"

"They're maintaining the planet. In case anyone needs to return."

Eurydike put her pistol away. "Humanity has always wondered why we've never contacted other civilizations. Perhaps it's because they've gone . . . inside . . . as well.''

"I've heard that theory voiced, yes.''

Lamoral scowled down at Sulejman. "And what about *you*, your majesty?''

"Me?''

"What are you doing on this planet when you could be off having adventures in alternate realities?''

Sulejman puffed on his cigaret. "My ambitions were never very high, I suppose, and my imagination is limited. As it happens, I've never wanted to be anything but King of Albania.''

"Even though your subjects are robots.''

Sulejman cleared his throat modestly. "It *does* make the job easier, you know. And I'm afraid I've never been very good at reigning over real people.''

Eurydike joined Lamoral on the table. "How many people are left on Earth?''

"A few million. People like me, without any imagination. Old people whose use for adventure is limited. Academics, eccentrics, historians. The Party Set is quite widely studied for anthropological reasons. That was the purpose of the unfortunate robot now resting in your deep freeze. It was recording you for study later.'

"Rats in a maze,'' Lamoral said. "That's all the Party Set is now.''

"Forgive me for suggesting this,'' stubbing out his cigaret, "but that's all the Party Set has *ever* been.''

"There has been a very elaborate charade,'' Lamoral said, "all designed to convince the Set that there has been no fundamental change, that all is as we wish it to be.'' He looked at Sulejman as if over the barrel of a gun. "Things will henceforth change.''

Sulejman was alarmed. "Great heavens! The control can't *know* it's a control. That would destroy its entire purpose.''

"The control,'' said Lamoral, "has the only pistols in this room.''

Sulejman thought for a moment, then came to the conclusion that silence was the better part of valor.

"Things will change,'' Lamoral repeated. "The Party Set

is going to have to be informed of a few things. They're the inheritors of the planet Earth, and I intend to see they receive their inheritance.''

Sulejman said nothing.

"And, since I presume most Party Set stock is now in the hands of caretaker robots, the robots will be instructed to vote out the current board of directors and vote in one of my choosing.''

Sulejman blanched. "How am I to arrange this?'' he said. "My influence extends only to one small part of the planet.''

"Presumably you know who's running things. Inform them of the changes I desire.''

"You can't wave pistols at *them*, your highness.''

"I can point the Party Set between their eyes and pull the trigger. Think about that.''

Sulejman took a long, ragged breath. "I'll tell them.''

"Good.'' Sulejman reached for another cigaret. Lamoral took Eurydike's hand, kissed the knuckles, returned the hand to its owner.

"And now, your majesty,'' he said, "you will now help me take the late Flight Officer Ram to my VTO, from which we will toss it in the Baltic Sea.''

Sulejman shuddered. "If you insist.''

"I do. I insist on everything. Remember that.''

Sulejman's eyes were filled with resignation. "Whatever you want, your serene highness.''

Lamoral smiled thinly. "I think I'm not Serene anymore. I rather think I've become a Royal.''

Alex's memorial service took place in the marble-walled chapel of the Hall of Sleep. Mary Maude Mullen, no longer Doyenne, dressed entirely in black, was mourning for much more than Alex.

"I should write a tragedy about her,'' Unger said. "A verse play. The good queen, brought low by one of her subjects.''

Lamoral looked at him. "Why not make it a farce?'' he said.

Unger turned, surveyed him carefully. He seemed unusually sober. "Your loss forgives you your sin, my son,'' he said.

"What forgives you yours?"

Unger thought for a ponderous moment. "Nothing," he decided. "Nothing at all."

He wandered off in the direction of the bar. Lamoral went on shaking hands and accepting condolences. What interesting realities, he thought, these intelligent, sophisticated people could create once they were liberated from their current illusion and allowed to construct their own.

Mary Maude Mullen, frail in her mourning cloth and black pearls, was the last. He clasped her black kid hand.

"I hope you will take care of my hounds and bitches," she said. "Managing them is not easy. Sometimes they bite."

"I've noticed."

Her eyes searched his face. "There has been one palace coup, young man. There will be another. I'll sleep till then."

"I wish you pleasant dreams in your icicle Avalon."

"And I am sorry about Alex, believe me. He had promise."

"So he did. I thank you."

Lamoral left the chapel and walked down soft carpets to the Doyenne's—the Doyen's—office. A brass plate had been affixed to the door, with the Thurn und Taxis arms, towers, the angel, and dead dog. He gazed at it for a moment, then opened the door.

Behind the desk was his throne, gold and scarlet, removed from the palace at Regensburg.

Eurydike looked up from one of the chairs. Pastel dogs gazed down at her. "That was a lovely service," she said.

"So it was. Pity we can't tell the truth about what happened up there."

"I should like Edwardes' name to be cleared sooner or later."

"It will be. Sooner or later." He stepped up to her. "What pocket universe will you wish to live in, once you have the choice?"

"One in which I am Princess of the Ghegs. I will be quite happy there for the next eon or so."

"Thank you." He kissed her. She smiled.

He turned to the fireplace and threw some logs on the embers. Then he took the poker and gazed at the shelves of porcelein.

This had needed doing for a long time.

The ones that wouldn't shatter he threw on the fire. His gift, and Alex's, went with the rest. Finished, winded and perspiring, he sat on the red velvet cushion and exchanged satisfied smiles with Eurydike.

A voice came from the comm unit. "His Albanian Majesty wishes to speak with you, sir."

"Let him in."

Sulejman stepped through the door, feet crunching on porcelain, and froze, looking at the ruin in shock.

Lamoral smiled at him.

"How do you like my doggies?" he said.

THE TOR DOUBLES

Two complete short science fiction novels in one volume!